Sundays
are for
hangovers

Mandy,
XOXO *[signature]*

♡ *[signature]*

K WEBSTER
J.D. HOLLYFIELD

Dedication

To Björk
(the devil pussy)

Sorry about that one time in the bathroom...

Mr. Wonka: "Don't forget what happened to the man who suddenly got everything he wanted."

Charlie Bucket: "What happened?"

Mr. Wonka: "He lived happily ever after."

—Roald Dahl, Charlie and the Chocolate Factory

For nearly a year, they've been at war.

Cops. Forks. Eggs.

Two feuding neighbors who couldn't be more opposite, forced to live next door to one another.

Neither is backing down.

She drives him crazy with her loud nineties rap music.

He gets under her skin the way he obsesses over his stupid perfect lawn.

She fantasizes about having sex with the hot nerd—but with duct tape over his dumb mouth.

He has dirty dreams of the bombshell beauty where he bangs the crazy right out of her—nightmares of course.

Anger isn't the only thing heating up between these two.

They think this is a battle only one of them can win...

The growing attraction between them, though, seems to be far more stubborn than the two of them combined.

Dear Reader,

We hope you enjoy our book!

Love,

K Webster & J.D. Hollyfield

Chapter One
Will

Sundays are for Yardwork

I squat to inspect one of the heads of my in-ground sprinkler system that's not spraying like it's supposed to. *What the fuck?* Two years ago, I paid forty-seven hundred dollars for this system so it would water my yard like clockwork while I'm at work. It's on a timer and everything. So why the hell is this head acting up? I push my black-rimmed glasses up my nose and squint.

It's jammed.

I pull my knife from my gym shorts pocket and flip it open. Something brown is hardened on one side. I pick and pick at it until I see bright pink underneath.

No fucking way.

A growl rumbles through me as I whittle away at the gunk. *Gum.* It's gum on my goddamned sprinkler head. As if on cue, music blasts from the house next door and I cringe.

Lilith Hamilton.

Instead of a homewrecker, she's a *neighborhood* wrecker. I swear the value of my house dropped at least fifteen grand the moment she pulled up in her cherry-red convertible Mustang with her oversized sunglasses perched on the end of her upturned nose. I remember the day—a year

1

ago—when she climbed out of her sporty car, blew a big pink bubble, and trampled all over my fire and ice hostas to introduce herself. I'd bitched her out for ruining my plants and *that* is how it's been ever since.

Her ruining the neighborhood and me trying to do damage control.

Fury bubbles up inside me as I scrape her gum from the sprinkler head. As I listen to Tupac's "California Love" blaring from her backyard, I want to turn the knife on myself and carve out my eardrums.

I can't take this anymore.

I've done everything including resorting to calling the cops.

She just charms them with her big, flirtatious grins. Shows a little cleavage and gets her way. *With them.* I am immune to her bullshit. My tolerance level for her obnoxious behavior is low and nearly every day I'm going off on her for some reason or another.

I want her gone.

And fuck how I've tried.

You'd think being the president of the Sprawling Oaks Neighborhood Homeowner's Association would give me some pull. Nope. She's not doing anything illegal and she pays her dues, so I can't exactly issue a lien on her property or call the city on her. I'm out of ideas and it's pissing me off. With a huff, I scoop up the hardened remains of her gum and stalk through my yard around the side of my house. I reach her gate and bang on the wood.

"Lilith!" I yell.

The song on the radio changes to "Big Poppa" by The Notorious B.I.G. and I lose it. She doesn't even have good taste in music. It's fucking maddening. I yank her gate open and storm into her backyard.

"Hey, Willy!" she chirps and raises her glass to me.

My gaze, against my will, rakes across her body as she bakes in the sun. Her tits are divine in a bright orange two-piece bikini that leaves little to the imagination and makes her skin more golden than usual. It's distracting sometimes that she's hot. Really fucking distracting.

"Bloody Mary, neighbor?" She grins at me and my blood boils. Her messy dark brown hair is piled up in a wild bun that fits her personality. Those lips—*fuck, those lips*—are painted a brilliant crimson that have dirty thoughts running through my mind at rapid speed.

Focus, Will, goddammit.

"This," I bark as I charge over to her and hold my fist out. "You left this in my sprinkler head." My tone drips with sarcasm.

Her nose scrunches up and she lifts her sunglasses to inspect what's in my palm. "Ew, sick. Keep your dirt in your flowerbeds. I don't want to see that."

"It's *your* gum," I snap.

She lets out a laugh that has her full tits jiggling with the movement. Again, fucking distracting. "Oops."

I glower at her, but she's nonplussed. "Keep your gum out of my yard. And do something about your weigela. It's overgrown and an eyesore."

She jerks her head down and inspects between her thighs, which makes *me* inspect between her thighs.

Fuck. Fuck. Fuck.

"There is nothing wrong with my weigela," she shrieks. "It's maintained quite nicely, I can assure you." She stares up at me and points at my face. "Keep your dirty mouth and your dirty hands in your dirty yard, Wonka."

Apparently she thinks it's cute calling me some variation of Willy Wonka from *Charlie and the Chocolate Factory*—since my name is William—because she does it all the damn time. It's not cute. It's annoying.

I blink at her in shock. Has she gone fucking mad? "Your *what*? Jesus, Lilith, I'm talking about the big, overgrown flowering shrub that's slowly creeping into my yard."

"Oh! Well, why are you calling it fancy names for a vagina then?" Her brows are furled together as if she's mad at me.

Are you kidding me right now?

This woman is going to give me a heart attack.

Grandma will have to bury her only family left because my nutty neighbor drove me to the grave at the early age of thirty-three.

I'll move. That's the only solution. I'll find someplace else where I don't have to deal with uncaring neighbors who blast nineties rap and drink alcohol on Sunday mornings and bring down neighborhood value with their unkempt yard and inconsideration of others.

"Your eye is twitching," she says as she adjusts her top. Her nipples are peaked and hard. It's not the only thing that's hard.

With a clenched jaw, I toss her gum remains onto the concrete beside her and storm over to her radio. I flip the channel to WXOJ because at least they play good music. Nirvana's "All Apologies" blares as I stride out of her backyard.

"What an asshole!"

I smirk, knowing I got to her by changing the station. I've barely made it into my own yard before "No Diggity" blasts from the speakers. But somehow, I feel as though I

4

won this round. It's hard to rile her up. She's so laissez-faire. Unfuckingcaring about anything but her stupid car and her stupid rap music.

My phone vibrates in my pocket and I answer harshly, "What?"

"Someone needs a Snickers." Grandma chuckles on the other line.

I groan, knowing I was rude to the woman I love most in this world.

"Sorry about that," I mutter. "I was dealing with a complicated matter."

She baby talks to her dog, Skippy, before chirping, "Complicated *female* matters?"

As a matter of fact, yes.

But I'm not telling Grandma that. She'll be over here in fifteen minutes flat with a wedding planner and a list of possible names for her future great-grandchildren. I thought Grandma was going to disown me when Presley and I broke up two years ago. My longtime girlfriend and I were on the path to marriage. Three years of dating. Two seemingly compatible people. And I even helped her pick out a puppy. Our five-year plan was underway. But three years in, she tossed in the towel. Just up and quit on me. Said I was too rigid and it wasn't working out.

Me.

Rigid.

I am not fucking rigid.

"It's a female," Grandma says knowingly. "What's her name?"

I clomp up my steps on my porch and walk inside, seeking the cold blast of my AC. My eyes scan my immaculate living room and pride swells inside of me. The white chenille blanket lies just the way I'd left it and my charcoal-gray cat Björk sits on top. Everything looks perfect. Straight from a magazine. Presley liked to *use* that decorative blanket when she stayed over. Curl up in it and complain about the temperature. It used to grate on my nerves like you would not believe. And worse yet, she always wore a smirk that said, "I know you don't like this, but I'm doing it anyway."

It's a decorative blanket and not to be used.

Ever.

Except by Björk, of course.

"William Grant. What's gotten into you?"

I let out a heavy sigh and sit in my leather recliner, relishing in the way it cools my sweaty back. "I'm just pissed at the neighbor. Her gum was stuck in the head of my—"

"Oooh," she coos, "the gorgeous bombshell neighbor?"

"Yes, I mean, no, she's not a bombshell, Grandma." I huff. "She's a *bomb*."

"Oh, don't be ridiculous, hon. She is a bombshell. Back in my day, I had curves like her and your grandfather used to—"

"Grandma!"

"My point is, you're blind if you don't notice the gorgeous woman who lives next door to you." She sighs dreamily and I roll my eyes. "She's much prettier than that Presley you were seeing."

I tense at the reminder. It's true. Lilith is all curves and color and practically drips sex. Presley was pastels and country club weekends and I-don't-give-blowjobs-because-that's-what-prostitutes-do. They're about as opposite as opposite can be. And despite Presley up and leaving me, *she* is my type.

Not irresponsible, loud, mouthy, messy hurricane types.

Those types do my head in.

I used to look forward to the weekends where I could unwind and do some yardwork. Sundays are for yardwork, after all. But now, I count down the minutes until Monday, where I can sit in my ten-by-ten-foot office and flip through mountains of documentation as I make sense of numbers. I hunt for holes and errors and fraud. I'm the senior internal bank auditor at Huffington Bank and Trust, which is Morristown, New Jersey's largest and most profitable local bank.

"You're too tense, hon," Grandma says, jerking me from my mental vacation. "Come over and have dinner with me. I made your favorite."

I scrub my palm over my sweaty face. "I'd love to, but can I get a raincheck? I have some things to do around here and I wasted all morning fixing my sprinkler head."

"Fine," she concedes. "But I want to see you this week. You need to relax. Maybe do some yoga."

Yoga.

My neck still hurts from the last time I tried to do Grandma's yoga. She made me go to her yoga class filled with a bunch of giggling old ladies months ago and she's been trying to get me to go back ever since. The yoga instructor, Lupe, was gay and made eyes at me the entire time. It was awkward. Really fucking awkward.

"I'll do some yoga," I agree just to get her off my back.

"I'll have Lupe email you some how-to videos," she assures me.

"Grandma, don't give him my email—"

"Love you!"

Click.

I toss my phone on the coffee table and rise from my

chair. I'm full of pent-up energy because my neighbor drives me insane. Maybe I should do some yoga.

Or get laid.

I can't even remember the last time I had sex. Maybe six months ago? I'd gone out with some guys from work and ended up screwing one of their sisters. One too many shots and I woke up with a mountain of regrets. The sex was mediocre at best and I had to spend the next six months avoiding Tom at the office.

That is why I don't drink often.

Those moments are few and far between, a far cry from my carefully and normally defined life.

A hot shower and a hand job will calm me the hell down. I peel off my shirt and saunter through the house. Once upstairs, I pass by the windows that overlook both our backyards and stop dead in my tracks. Lilith has turned onto her stomach to sun her back. Her very naked back. The tiny scrap of her bikini top is tossed on the concrete nearby.

My cock jerks in my shorts and I groan.

Why does she have to be so fucking hot?

An annoyed grumble escapes me as I try to peel my gaze away from her round ass. Her orange swimsuit bottoms have ridden up the crack of her ass and show off her toned glutes. If I didn't hate her so much, I'd ask her how she stays so in shape. Her thighs are muscular and her calves are like fists of muscle hidden behind her tanned flesh.

I close my eyes and let my mind imagine what all her curves look like without her swimsuit. My cock aches and I refrain from rubbing one out while creepily thinking about my hot-ass neighbor. It takes an incredible amount of strength, but I manage to pry myself away from the window and all but run to the shower.

As the spray of the water runs through my hair, I grip my cock and allow myself one dirty selfish moment. A moment where I imagine Lilith's bright red lips wrapped around my dick. I fuck her face and she likes it. But then my mind tries to blend my fantasy with my nightmare. My cock grows soft as I think about her stupid pink gum stuck in my pubes.

Goddamn you, Lilith, you're even ruining my masturbation time.

I can't get away from this girl.

Something has to change.

Fuck.

Chapter Two

Lilith

Tuesdays are for Pink Tacos

"I know, Mother." I roll my eyes, knowing if she saw me through the phone, she'd likely smack the disobedient look right off my face.

"Lilith, dear, you know how your father is. He just wants to see you succeed."

And I want to see myself be at work on time. "I *know*, Mother."

"And please, return Lance's calls. His mother told me he's been trying to get in touch for a gathering and you seem to always be busy."

Ugh…she's hitting all the topics today, isn't she? First my father and then the loser they keep trying to set me up with. "Mother, I *am* busy. Work is super busy right now."

The sigh on the other end can be heard around the world. Anytime I bring up my job, being a radio jockey for a local station, it makes my mother's skin crawl. To think her own flesh and blood, Lilith Hamilton, daughter to the elite, hoity-toity Bart and Tonya Hamilton spends her time mingling with blue-collar people, playing records, and tarnishing the family name probably keeps her up at night.

"Lilith, playing around on the radio all day isn't work.

It's a hobby. You know you must pick a real career soon. Your father offered the senior analyst position to you if you would just come home and stop this silly little rebellious journey you're on."

That silly journey is pretty much my life. Thanks, Mom. "It's not a journey. A radio jockey gets paid great." Lies. "And people depend on me." I may have laughed at that one myself. "So, you tell Daddy I'm not taking the job. I'm happy where I'm at right now."

I've been on the phone for the past ten minutes, standing outside the radio station listening to her whine and moan that Daddy Dearest doesn't approve of my choices. But he never has. Not since the day I took off a year ago, landing in Morristown, New Jersey. I was your typical A-lister. Top of my class dressed in pristine Valentino bubblegum pink dresses. I was exactly what my parents wanted me to be.

Perfect.

Sadly, I wanted to be the opposite.

There was no way I saw my life going down the path my parents did. They had every detail planned, but I had dreams to travel, make my own choices, and just be me. When I approached my father, I pleaded with him to give me time. Allow me the opportunity to be on my own. Spread my wings. Blossom into the woman I was meant to become. The answer the first million times was no, despite me being a grown-ass woman. It varied into different versions, but the overall outcome all meant the same. I have a feeling it took some pushing from my mother for him to finally agree. As stoked as I was that he was finally agreeing to let me go, it wasn't without stipulations. The important one being, I had one year. One year to get the nonsense out of my system. I knew that wouldn't be enough. But at the time, I agreed. I took what I could get and thought I'd figure it all out when the time came. The problem is, that year is officially up.

I take a peek at my watch, knowing I'm cutting it real close. The door to the studio opens and Daryl, or his radio jockey nickname, Big D, sticks his head out, signaling I have two minutes before I go on. Since we've been working together for the past year, I give him my universal, 'on the phone with my mother, shoot me, gag me, okay, I'll be right in' stare. And, yes, he got all that.

"Mother, really, I have to go. I'm on air in two minutes. Tell Daddy to go hire someone else. I love you and we'll talk next week." As in tomorrow since that's when she'll call me back to have this exact conversation all over again. I'm about to hang up, but I can still hear her yapping away.

"Lilith, dear, wait. Are you coming to brunch next Sunday? The Petersons will be attending. Lance will be there!"

Well, then you have that answer.

Nope with a nope on top.

When I escaped my parents' fancy chains and the social society, elite bullshit, I also escaped the nerdy googly eyes of Lance Peterson. When you're born and raised in my lineage, which is power, prestige, money, and more money, your parents believe they know best on how your life's going to pan out. Mine knew exactly what I was going to do in life, that being, to work at my father's ridiculously successful worldwide investment company, Hamilton Investments. I was to fall in love with their best friends' son and have tons of regal babies and live the remainder of my days as the lady of the house, probably on my parents' estate so they would never have to fully get their claws out of me. I'm sure the only reason Daddy wants me to take the job is to be closer to Lance, so he can propose on my first day, then insist I don't dirty my pretty little hands and stay home.

Gag.

Still gagging!

I tell her, we'll see, and hang up just as I throw the studio door open. I land my ass in my chair and pull on my headphones with attached mic.

"*Goood* morning, Morristown! Coming to you as fresh as your morning coffee, it's the Lil and Big D show. If you're alive and made it past Monday, then congrats to you. We're gonna reward you with Tacobout it Tuesday. Now we all know Tuesdays were invented merely as an excuse to eat tacos. That's why Manny's on Jefferson offers half-off tacos between five and midnight! Make sure to tell 'em Lil and Big D sent ya. Now, let's talk some Tuesday traffic, but first, here's some Nirvana's 'Lithium' for your morning commute."

I click off the *Live on Air* button and pull my headphones off my ears.

"Your momma handin' you the ultimatums again?" Daryl asks, setting his headset next to him, scratching at his wiry beard.

"When is she not?" I ask with a huff. "It's like she *wants* me to never come home, mentioning fancy dinner dates and the L-word."

Daryl laughs, his giant belly jiggling with the movement. He knows what the L-word stands for. Lance. Dorky Lance and his horrible comb-over and ritzy lawyer job and all his boring, snooze-fest attributes. I cringe just at the thought of having to sit through a boring brunch, with not only my uptight parents, but their uptight friends, and their uptight son. I'd rather get doused in taco sauce and set myself on fire than sit at one of those.

Ouch. That kinda sounds painful—

"What's the sour look for?"

"Uh, nothing. So, we still on for tacos at Manny's after work? I really want to try and beat my tequila and taco record. Feel like tonight's gonna be the night." Since we promote Manny's taco and salsa bar, Manny, the owner, hooks us up. Not that we can't afford half-off tacos, but since Daryl can take down enough to feed a small colony, the discount helps. Have I mentioned we're also on a jockey salary?

"Girl, that place owns my heart."

I laugh. Because if there is one thing Big D loves more than razzing people on the radio, it's eating. Which I second, because what goes best with tacos?

Tequila.

Daryl and I walk into Manny's, and no surprise, it's packed.

"This town sure does love them some discounted tacos," Daryl points out, wincing as he walks, his bad knee giving him problems. He isn't lying either. The place is packed. It's also because Manny, when opening the joint, attached a salsa dance club to it. So not only do you get your tacos, you get to dance them off too. Well, not Daryl and his bad knee. He just watches from the sidelines.

We head to our normal spot, a nice reserved sign on a bar table waiting for us. We'd probably have to be dead or close to it to miss out on Taco Tuesday. While getting comfortable, we spot Manny and wave. It's our universal sign for 'we've arrived, bring us the goods.' In no time, we'll have a full table of double trouble. Tacos and tequila.

"So, have you thought about what we talked about?"

Daryl starts in.

"What? The Tinder app? No. I really don't want to get murdered just because I'm desperate and need my weigela played with."

"Your what?"

"Oh, sorry, my weigela. A word my nerdy neighbor made up for my vagina. Well, not my vagina, my plant, but that weirdo probably wished it were my vagina." Not that I also didn't wish, since minus the glasses and pole stuck so far up his tight ass, he's super-hot. Not that I pay attention.

"Neighbor, huh? Thought you despised that dude?"

A waitress comes over to our table and sets down a tray of chips, salsa, and four shots of tequila. We're already downing the first one before she's even away from our table.

"I do. The guy's so anal, he sometimes cuts his lawn with a pair of scissors if the mower missed a spot. Always nagging. I tell ya, he might need a sexual release more than I do." And that is no lie. Ever since the moment I moved in, the guy next door has been a pain in my ass. I've attempted to be nice. I've invited him over for drinks, music, sun tanning. You name it. I've even asked if he wanted to hand cut *my* lawn, which by the way, I thought was being kind since he looked so damn into it.

We grab for the second shots of tequila, clink, and down 'em.

"You should just fuck your neighbor."

That causes me to choke, almost wasting a good shot. I choke it down, my eyes wide as saucers. "Ew, no! He'd probably complain the entire time we were doing it. *Trash day really needs to be twice a week. Speaking of, stop putting your trash in my bin. Oh yeah, a little more to the right. Oh yes... do me, do me..."*

We both start laughing. It's not that I haven't accidently imagined myself doing my neighbor. I can't deny he's smokin' hot. He's an avid runner, so he's super in shape. A little psycho about it, though, since he sometimes runs twice a day. It's just his damn mouth. I also won't deny it either that in my fantasy I'm riding him nasty style with a piece of duct tape over his mouth.

"Why not? He's good-looking. Maybe a set of contacts wouldn't hurt." Daryl laughs at his poke.

I shove a chip in my mouth. "I don't know. The glasses don't really bother me. It's his stupid mouth that does. If he would just shut up and stop complaining for once, I'd totally be into him. I mean, it's like he wasn't held enough as a child or something. Never satisfied. Plus, he hates me. Which is fine, 'cause I'm no fan of his either."

Will Grant, aka the nerdy neighbor, is just not on my radar. He's exactly the type of guy I'm running far away from. The uptight, bowtie wearing, snooty kinda guy who's probably so boring that when he beats off, his poor dick falls asleep.

Not sure why I'm even thinking about his dick. I bet it's big, though. I've seen that bad boy jammed into his running shorts bouncing. Ahh, the things I could teach that guy.

"So fine, no neighbor. You going to download the app or what? Boo, you *need* to get laid. And if it's not gonna be by your hot uptight neighbor, then go swipe right to some random."

Both sound unappealing. Daryl is convinced I need to get laid. I'm *also* convinced, but I'm not really a one-night stand kinda girl. Not that there haven't been any. Just none I'll admit to or discuss.

I'd just rather find a guy I like. Go on a date. Maybe flirt a little bit before I show him my thong collection and moan his name in pure delight till the early morning. But in this day and age, that seems impossible. "Nah, I'm good. I'll just try and find someone the old-fashioned way. Maybe Manny has a brother he can hook me up with."

We both laugh as a gentleman approaches us.

"Hi, you two," says Jack Stone, otherwise known as our town fire chief.

"Hey, Fireman Jack. What's up?" I raise my hand and force him to high five me. He's resistant at first but follows through. Win for me.

Jack frowns at me, a bit uncomfortable. "Nothing much, but, Lilith, I wanted to let you know we received another anonymous call about your house not being up to code with fire detectors."

Daryl laughs as my mouth falls open.

"Dude, seriously? You guys were just out last month checking because of the first call."

"I know. But if we receive a call, we have to come check."

Last month the fire department got a call from an anonymous caller, stating they were concerned over the outdated fire detectors in my home and insisted someone come check them before I set the neighborhood on fire. Of course, the detectors were up to code, because despite my parents who think I live in the ghetto compared to their pristine home, I do live in a nice house. I wished them a good day and spent the rest of the afternoon making a list of who had it out for me enough to make that call. Until it clicked.

Will Grant.

"Clearly this is bullshit. And we all know who called."

Jack's sympathetic eyes tell me he also knows. "Sorry,

Lil, but it's our job. I just thought I'd warn you. Someone from the firehouse will be by sometime this week or next for a run-through."

He shakes Daryl's hand, complimenting today's show, and then he's gone.

"That fucking weasel!"

"Maybe he only wants to make sure you're safe." Daryl won't stop laughing.

"More like he keeps trying to find ways to get rid of me." I'm fuming. To think I even considered playing nice with him and his junk. Fuck that. Four more shots are brought to our table and I slam two, the alcohol an accelerant on my anger.

Who does he think he is trying to mess with me like that?

If he wants to play, then fine.

Two can play this game.

"Girl, you are too drunk. Maybe wait until tomorrow to steal 'em." Daryl is pulling into my driveway. We spent the entire night conjuring up ideas for revenge and I figured out the perfect one. It's simple. When I get home, which it's currently rolling on two in the morning, I'm going to walk over with a handful of tacos, salsa, and some fancy drink Manny sent me home with and offer a truce. I'm going to ask to come in and use the bathroom. And after he thanks me profusely for all the tacos, I'm going to go inside and steal his fire detector. Then, while he lies in bed thinking about how wonderful I am and how delish Manny's tacos were, I'll make a simple call to the firehouse claiming to be a concerned neighbor. Even Steven.

"No way. I'm good. Who will say no to taaaacooooos?" I start laughing. *Tacccoooos*. I should tell him I have a special pink taco back at my place if he's interested. I start to laugh even harder at myself.

"Yeah. You need to go to bed, girl." He grabs for me when I start to get out.

"No!" I throw the door open and wobble out, trying to juggle the mound of food and drink in my hand. "This is happening." I turn, using my buns of steel to push the door shut, and I make my way next door.

I start singing as I dance across his pristine lawn. "If you like piña coladas…" I start shaking my butt. "Or getting lost in the—"

Mid line, something from the ground pops up, and the entire lawn starts spraying water.

"AHHH!" I squeal, getting shot in the face by flying water. I realize the neighbor's sprinklers are going off and run to get off his lawn.

That's when I slip.

And my legs go up in front of me.

And all the food goes flying.

In an unladylike fashion, I fall on my ass, with a shower of Mexican food to follow.

"Oh my God." I look around at the heaps of ruined Mexican food littering Will's lawn. "The poor tacos," I whine. I'm trying to cover my face from getting shot with water. I attempt to get up but slide on a destroyed taco, smashing it into the grass and falling back down onto the cup of salsa. The container breaks under me, splattering everywhere. I groan thinking I would have still eaten the salsa even with a little bit of water in it.

One more attempt to get up and another no go. It's like a Jell-O wrestling match. I'm sliding all over the wet tacos, smearing them into the lawn, failing every time I try to stand.

Thankfully Daryl finally comes to my rescue, pulling me up and half carrying me back to my house. For a fleeting moment, I worry about his bad knee.

"Okay, so maybe you're right. Let's wait until tomorrow to get even." I lick sour cream and grass off my fingers, then push through the door, bidding him good night as I barely get it closed behind me.

Chapter Three

Will

Wednesdays are for...
What the Fuck is on my Lawn?

I lace up my Nikes and crack my neck as I head out for my morning run. Running is something new to me. Presley is the one who got me into it. And while she gave up on it, just like everything else in her life, I kept it going. I run twice a day if I can. Early in the morning, it's refreshing and invigorating, every bit a part of my morning ritual as my black coffee and the daily crossword puzzle in the *Morristown Gazette*. I give Björk a pat on the head on my way out.

At five in the morning, nobody is hardly up yet and I get the neighborhood to myself. It's dark because I even beat the damn sun up. I'm grinning as I run across my grass toward the street, still looking up at the sky, pondering if I smell rain in the air when I slip. At first I think it's Mr. Paulson's dog shitting in my grass again. But another step and I slip again, falling hard on my ass.

The stench of Mr. Paulson's dog's ass is not what assaults my senses, though. Salsa. What the fuck is on my lawn? I lift a hand and chunks of goddamned salsa are left all over my palm. I jerk my head around to see the horror scene surrounding me. Destroyed tacos. Salsa. Crushed to-go containers. Tortilla chips.

I'm stunned.

Fucking stunned.

With an enraged growl, I stand and glare at the mess. I don't even have to follow the trail to know who's responsible. Same nutty neighbor who's responsible for everything horrible in my life. I storm over to my extra-long water hose and start blasting her mess back over into her yard. It takes far too long and the sun starts to peek over the horizon by the time I'm satisfied. I'm positively fuming.

You know what?

Fuck this girl.

With my hose in hand, I stomp over to her house.

Bangbangbangbangbang!

Bangbangbangbangbang!

Bangbangbangbangbang!

Bangbangbangbangbang!

Bangbangbangbangbang!

Bangbangbangbangbang!

"Oh my God! Shut the hell up!" she mutters from just inside the door.

I twist the knob and am surprised to find it unlocked. For a brief moment it makes me want to run home and locate the safety statistics we discussed in the last Homeowner's Association meeting. This may be a nice neighborhood, but those are the places criminals often prey upon. A single woman like herself is vulnerable and—

You know what?

Fuck this girl. Fuck her so hard.

I push the door open and find her sprawled out on the floor. Her clothes are soiled and she reeks of tequila. Fury bubbles to explosive levels and I lose my mind. Pointing my hose at her, I unleash the beast. Water surges into her house, specifically spraying her.

"WHAT THE HELL?!" she screeches as she tries to scramble to her feet. Her drunk ass tries several times before she makes it up.

I release the trigger on my hose, toss it behind me, and snap at her. "Keep your chaos over here where it belongs," I roar. "Stay off my fucking lawn."

Her surprise molds into rage. She picks up a vase nearby and launches it at me. It misses me and sails over my head onto her porch, shattering behind me. "You're such an over-bearing psycho!" she yells as she charges for me.

She slips in the water and slams against my chest. On instinct, I grab her hips to keep her from falling. Her fingers have fisted my shirt and she glares up at me. For a moment, I'm caught off guard, staring into her pretty brown eyes. They flare with anger but then soften as she regards me. It has me calming considerably just looking at her gorgeous features up close.

"Why are you so messy?" I ask, my voice husky as I realize she's beautiful even soaked to the bone and stinking of salsa and tequila.

"Why are you so mean?" She bites on her bottom lip, looking innocent as hell, and it does me in.

I push her away slightly but don't release her hips. Now that I have a hold of her curves, my fingers aren't so eager to let them go. "You need to get this toweled up soon or it'll ruin the hardwood," I murmur.

She regards me silently for a moment. "Right. Okay, Willy."

Irritation has my spine straightening with resolve. I

reluctantly remove my hands from her body and step away. With her clothes molded to her tight little body, I physically react to her. Again. My cock thickens and that's my cue to leave. "I'm filing an official report with the HOA," I inform her as I sidestep the broken pottery on the porch.

"I'll be doing the same, wise guy."

I jerk around and glare at her. "You're the one who destroyed my lawn."

She motions to her soaked entryway. "And you soaked my house. Perhaps I should also file a report with the Morristown PD. Breaking and entering is a serious charge, Wonka. Really serious. Like they may even remove your Yard of the Month sign as punishment," she taunts. "Oh, the horror."

"Try it," I snarl, my chest heaving with fury. "Just fucking try it, demon."

She snorts. "Demon?"

"All I'm saying is stay the hell away from me and my grass."

Her eyes narrow at me. "Should I tell the cops you're also growing the ganja?"

"The what?"

"Weed, man. Grass. You're not helping your case the more you talk. It's like your lips are moving and a whole lot of lalalalalalalala comes out, but nobody understands what kind of bullshit you're speaking!"

"Hamilton," I warn.

"I'm serious, Willnotlightenthefuckup."

I open my mouth but snap it closed. Arguing with her is a moot point.

"That's the best thing you've said all day." She smirks before slamming the door.

When I walk into work, I'm on a rampage. It'd been on this month's agenda to audit the lending department and now I'm making it my priority. I stalk to my office and grab my clipboard. The clipboard. The thing that makes all these motherfuckers around here quiver in their damn loafers. I may not be the damn CEO, but I decide their fate. If they screw up, I'll find out about it. If they steal, I'll bring them to their knees. Not one figure or detail goes unnoticed.

"Drinks after work?" Joe Campbell, a customer service rep, questions as I pass his desk to the lending department.

Drinks and a bar fly.

Don't mind if I do.

Anything to get my mind off my crazy-ass neighbor and her bangin' body.

"Six sharp. The Voodoo Lounge. Find a tie or don't bother coming," I bark, barely sparing him a glance.

He laughs. "Can I borrow one of your bowties?"

I screech to a halt and glare at him. One of my only friends at this bank that is nonplussed at my furious reaction. He simply flashes his million-dollar smile that has made him the top performer in his department and shrugs. I roll my eyes at him and he snorts.

"Nobody can rock a bowtie like I can," I grumble as I straighten mine. Today it's red. Like Lilith-Daughter-of-the-Devil-Hamilton's dick sucking lips.

"Touché, man."

I pivot on my heel and storm past the teller line. The girls who work the windows are all young, around nineteen or so. I don't miss the way they regard me with equal parts fear and unhidden interest.

Nobody can rock a bowtie like I can.

I strut past them into Morgan Stewart's office. He's pushing eighty, but he's this bank's highest producing lender. Corporate loans are his niche. Sometimes I wonder what it is ol' Stewart does to make him so damn successful. Which is exactly why he's my first target today.

"Aww, shit," he mutters under his breath and leans back in his chair. "I thought audits for our department were later this month."

I stand near the edge of his desk, glowering down at him, and shake my head. I'm the sheriff of this town and they're all going to step in line or get out. I motion for the door with my thumb. "Go make loans."

He grunts as he rises from his chair and collects his coat. As soon as he's gone, I sit at his desk and start pulling out his files. From his computer, I log in to my profile and pull up my spreadsheet for his loans so I can begin my process of checking for inaccuracies. For the first time in days, I feel at peace.

"I fucked Tammy from the teller line," Joe tells me as he shoves a fresh bottle of beer across the table to me.

I'm not one to drink often, but Lilith is driving me straight to the bottle. I need to unwind and not think about her terrorizing my life.

"And what does HR think about you banging Tammy?" I ask, my tone dry.

He snorts. "What they don't know won't hurt them. What's got you in such a pissy mood anyway?"

I'm about to open my mouth to explain when I hear her

laugh. Loud and airy and genuinely happy. This morning she was throwing vases at me and whipping me with insults, yet now she's in my favorite lounge acting as though she doesn't have a care in the world.

"Her," I growl and lean out of the booth to catch a glimpse of my little nightmare across the bar.

Joe follows my gaze and hisses. "Hot damn. Is she your girl?"

"What? Fuck no," I snap. "She's my annoying-ass neighbor."

"More like I want to tap that ass neighbor. Seriously, Will. How can you live next door to that and not want to hit it?"

She's wearing a dress you'd see on a fifties pinup. Black with white polka dots and the tallest blood-red fuck me heels I've ever seen. The dress is short and every time she bends down to pat some big guy on the shoulder, she gives Joe and me a great view of her tanned thighs. My cock thickens in my work slacks and I groan.

"Stop looking at her ass," I grumble. "She's the devil."

"I'd fuck the devil if she came with a pair of heels like that."

My blood boils, mostly because I don't want him checking out her ass. I want him to agree with me she's a psycho who lives to drive me fucking crazy.

Just then, she turns and our eyes collide. I'm caught staring her down. Her eyes widen for a moment and her pouty red lips are parted in surprise. My gaze travels down her low-cut dress. Her cleavage is perky and on full display for everyone to see. Joe needs to put his fucking tongue back in his mouth before I yank it out and stomp on it.

"Wonka, what are you doing here?" she demands, her

hands going to her waist. The same waist I had my own hands on earlier today.

"Wonka?" Joe asks in confusion.

"Forget it," I growl at him. I pin her with a harsh stare. "This is my bar."

She frowns. "I thought Eddie Chambers owned it." She yells over her shoulder, "Eddie? You sell this joint and forget to tell your favorite customer?"

"No, Lil," he calls back from behind the bar. "She's all mine."

Her lips purse together and she winks at me. "I must have misheard." She waltzes over to our booth, her tits bouncing with her movement. When she reaches me, she tugs at my bowtie. "This is my bar, Willy."

I grip her wrist and pull her hand away from me, but I can't let her go for some reason. "Well, on Wednesdays, it's my bar now. You can have the other days of the week."

"Is hot Peewee Herman giving you trouble?" the big guy sitting at her table questions.

"Nah, D, I've got him." Her brown eyes sear into mine and she licks her lips. "You should go. You're not wanted here."

I tug her until she's forced to sit beside me. The scent of tequila and salsa is gone. Now, she smells sweet. Like fucking wisteria. It's fitting since she's an invasive species—one that plants her roots, overtakes, and chokes out the neighboring plants.

My cock disagrees.

My cock thinks she's hot as sin and he wants to play in her garden, even if she's a little poisonous.

"You're walking on thin ice, woman," I utter low enough for only her to hear. My eyes, against my wishes, flit

ParseА

down to her exposed cleavage and I suppress a groan. I bet they taste like heaven. But all the things that'll kill you in the end always do.

"Good thing I took figure skating in college," she bites back.

My brows scrunch together as I search her eyes. "Wait? Seriously?"

She smiles broadly at me and for a moment, I'm stunned by how fucking innocent she looks. "It was only a few lessons because I had it bad for the instructor. A few falls on my ass and a broken tailbone later, I decided it didn't matter how cute he was…my ass was cuter. Would you know I had bruises for weeks?"

"And that's my cue to get us something stronger," Joe says, amusement in his voice as he vacates the booth.

Thoughts of her tanned ass littered with bruises do not help the state of my cock. What I wouldn't give to bend her over my knee and spank her disobedient ass.

"You're the only man I know who can pull off a bow-tie," she says, her voice soft.

I stare at her, searching for malice in her words. She's being truthful. It's then I realize my thumb is rubbing circles on her wrist. I jerk my hand away and pick up my beer.

"You stay to your half of the bar and I'll stay to mine," I grumble.

She lets out a huff and mutters that I'm an asshole.

Tell me something I don't know.

An hour flies by and I can't keep my eyes off her. She works the room like she was born to do it. Several guys are sitting at her table and I recognize one from television. Joe later points out he's the singer for Novahope, a band in town for a concert tomorrow. Stake is his name. Who the fuck names their kid Stake?

And Stake is staking his claim on *my* neighbor.

As she drinks like she's one of the boys, he gets more flirty and handsy with her. I've barely touched my first beer and I'm about to drain it so I can knock it over that emo fucker's head. What kind of asshole wears skinny jeans and a fauxhawk and thinks he can land a girl like Lilith? She's a classic beauty. A Natalie Woods from the sixties' *West Side Story* type of beauty. Voluptuous and unattainable by the likes of assholes named Stake.

He teases her by trying to pull the front of her dress down and peek at her tits. Over my dead fucking body. I slide out of the booth and stalk over to their table. Towering over Stake, I push his hand away from her and glare at him.

"She's taken," I growl. I'm irritated that I have to save her from herself and these idiots who clearly want to take advantage of her.

His eyes are wide. I could snap a little pre-pubescent turd like him in six seconds. You don't work out like it's your damn job not to be able to figuratively throw your weight around when the time arises. I have muscles this prick only dreams of having when he grows up one day. "What?"

"Will," she bites out, shaking her head. "No."

Ignoring her, I walk around to where she's sitting and haul her to her feet. She sways, the alcohol overtaking her, and I do what I should have done an hour ago. I squat and toss her over my shoulder.

"WILL!" she screeches.

I eyeball every motherfucker at her table, including the big guy who's laughing, and spit out, "I'm taking her home."

Some bar patrons cheer as I storm out with a furious pinup girl over my shoulder. She beats on my back but eventually gives up. It isn't until we're outside and the warm summer night air breezes past us that I set her on her feet. She's still unsteady on her feet, so I clutch onto her hips again. Fuck, I love her hips.

"You embarrassed me," she says, her bottom lip trembling. Tears well in her eyes and I feel like the biggest dick on the planet.

I blow out a huff of air, releasing the tension from my shoulders. I reach up and tuck a brown strand of her hair behind her ear. It's silky and I could spend hours stroking it. The thought is alarming.

"I'm sorry," I mutter. "I just didn't like that guy. He was touching you."

She lifts her chin in defiance. "And why is that your problem?"

My palm cups the side of her jaw and I run my thumb over her fat bottom lip. I pull it down and pinch it between my thumb and finger. "It just is, Lilith. It just fucking is."

Chapter Four

Lilith

Thursdays are for Revenge

I sleep like the dead.

Or I *should be* since Thursdays are my day off.

My phone has been beeping all morning and I want to throw it out the window. I've spent the last hour tossing and turning, trying to fight the rage building inside me at what my damn neighbor pulled last night. I'm not going to be shocked when I look at my messages and see the station bitching me out for what happened. I was supposed to be entertaining Novahope until super freak next door insulted Stake and threw me over his shoulder.

I should have told him to go suck it then and there, gone back inside and done damage control for me and the station, but instead I let my shitty day and the booze catch up to me which had me feeling emotional. It didn't help that just before he came barging in my house I had just gotten off the phone with my pesky mother with her tacky threats about me going home or my father coming and dragging me home.

In every call, she's made remarks about visiting me and that scares me even more. My mother would drop dead if she saw how I was living—a regular home in a regular non-gated subdivision. She knows nothing outside of her royal castle. Not to mention, when I had Daddy write the check for the house, I may have sent him a photo of some fancy place I had pinned on Pinterest, instead of the small little bungalow I'm currently living in. It's not that I wanted to lie, but my parents don't understand. My mother would have me sleeping in my pearls if she had a say. The way I dress would be unacceptable and she'd have her tailor over here in a flash, measuring me for chiffon gowns and organza suits. I just want to be me. And not them.

My day got even worse when I got to work and Daryl told me someone was trying to buy the station. When I asked who, and the name of my father's investment company rang through the air, I wanted to murder someone. There was nothing I could do without my father having a hand in it. Going as far as purchasing the place I work shouldn't even surprise me. I'm sure if the sale goes through he'd just shut the entire station down, giving me one more push to come home.

And to top it off, my neighbor thought he could jump in and tell me how I should let people handle me. Talk about not minding his own damn business. I wanted to smack the narcissistic smile right off him.

Who cares if he was kind on the way home? Even though the silent game isn't really considered being kind, but in this case, him not talking was doing a good justice for me.

I spent the ride repeating to myself that I had no interest in him whatsoever. Even if my body was still tingling at the way his hands were gripping my hips, his fingers brushing against my lower lip. There was only one way to explain the weird vibes my body was sending it.

And it was that I had lost it.

When we finally made it home, I jumped out of his car, which still smelled like—no shocker—a new car, and stormed off. I opened my door, slammed it shut for dramatics, and then slipped on the still wet rug from earlier. If I wasn't so damn butt hurt, *literally*, at how he got me back from the taco incident, I would've stormed right back over and laid into him. But I knew I had bigger plans of revenge for him.

My phone beeps again, making it the billionth and one time it's gone off. A loud, overdramatic grunt sounds up my throat. "Lord help me, because I don't look good in stripes." I throw myself across my Egyptian cotton, Serbian goose, down comforter. The fluffiest comforter known to man. I take a moment to snuggle my face into my best friend, then reach over and grab my phone. With one eye open, I start to scan through my missed texts.

Big D: You swipe right with your neighbor last night? Call me.

Big D: Girl, you better rein in your neighbor. You lying naked next to him still? He needs to back off. He called the station and put in a complaint.

"What the *fuck*?" I fly forward, sitting up in bed.

Bossman: Call me RIGHT NOW!

Big D: You're lucky I love you for all the fires I'm putting out for you.

Big D: Girl, your boytoy's gotta get checked. He be claimin' sexual harassment and

B-man ain't happy. Might wanna have a chat about that before you do the walk of shame home.

Big D: Novahope is still doing the concert and the pre-show interview. You're welcome.

Bossman: You better have a good reason for what went down last night.

Big D: Don't hate on me, but I did what I had to do. Love you, girl.

Bossman: Daryl told me about your womanly issues. Take the time you need.

Womanly issues?

Sexual harassment?

I'm going to KILL WILL!

I throw myself out of bed. A calmer person may put on pants before storming outside and across the lawn, but not me. I am livid!

Taking my closed fist, I bang on his door until I hear movement inside. My mind is flooding with every single threat and insult when the door opens.

"You fucking jerk! Who do you think you are? You called my work and placed a sexual harassment complaint?" I'm seeing red. And through those red shades my eyes see a man, covered in muscle. And the reason why I see all this muscle is because he's standing in front of me in only a pair of black boxers.

"That's all you have to say to me? Not a thank you for saving you from a creep who was practically molesting you in public?"

My red shade turns to a deep maroon. We're talking like blood red. Exactly what is about to be spilled when I rip his head off. "That *creep* was my client. It's my *job* to flirt with him. Show him a good time!"

He folds his arms over his sculpted chest. "So, it's your job to be assaulted?"

Oh my God!

This guy is off his rocker.

"I wasn't being assaulted, and for the record, no one asked you to get involved." My foot is tapping like a madman. I don't know what to do with my own hands. I go from crossing them over my chest to fighting not to lock 'em into his hair, tug him out of his house, and kick his ass on his own damn lawn.

"So, let me get this straight." He takes a step closer to me. "For a job, you allow strangers to touch you in ways only your man should? It's okay for them to hang on to you like this?" He unwraps his arms from his chest, placing his hands back to my hips, just like last night. "It's completely okay for a man to put you on his lap and let your tight little ass rub against his dick?"

Jesus, what?

I know he just said dick.

I know it's my turn to reply.

Maybe tell him to go take his own dick and fuck off, but my lips won't move.

They want to part, suck in air, but I'm experiencing some sort of malfunction. My brain is stalled at the fact that his hands are still on me. The word *dick* on repeat in my head doesn't help either. My eyes suddenly drop down past his chest. Two, four, six, yep all abs in place. My eyes don't stop there. His black boxers lie low on his hips, no doubt failing at hiding his morning wood. And, *Jesus*, I knew the guy was big. Like impressively big. I wonder if he has to tailor his pants to fit the big guy—

"See something you like?" His voice breaks the debate in my head, and I quickly pull my eyes off his goods.

"Ew, no! Seriously, Wonka? I wasn't looking at your junk. More like your dirty floors. Geez, clean much?"

His eyes light up in shock, followed by a distraught,

garbled sound coming from his throat. I knew that would do it. He lets me go, which, not gonna lie, bums me out, to inspect his floor. "My floor is not dirty. I just washed it yesterday. You could eat off this floor." He's still looking down, and I'm standing there waiting for him to drop to his knees with a magnifying glass in search of dirt.

"Whatever, just stay out of my business, got it?" I begin walking back to my house when he calls out to me.

"Is it also your job to run around the neighborhood exposing yourself? I'm sure the HOA frowns upon people walking around half naked."

I quickly look down, remembering, with no time to dress, I ran out of my house in my bra and underwear. And just to make the vision worse for me, better for him, I'm in a thong.

I throw my hands over my chest, then try covering my ass. Knowing I only have two hands, I decide he's already seen it all and make use of what I got by raising my middle finger and flicking him off.

"You shouldn't let men you don't know touch you like that," he states again while I walk with pride, chin high as can be while shaking my bare ass at him.

I turn to him while continuing to walk backward. "And why's that, Wonka? Men love girls like me. Nice and easy." There's a fire that flashes in his eyes. And it kinda turns me on. Why am I suddenly tempted to go back and let him have his way with me? I know he wants me. Morning wood doesn't last *that* long. I'm willing to admit I want him too. But sometimes two people just can't get along long enough to play nice. Which also seems to turn me on even more. Rage-filled, heated, passionate, nail scraping, biting, choking sex. Jesus, having hate sex with my neighbor would be super-hot.

"Did you want to say something else to me, Lilith?"

Yeah, I just fucked you three times in my head. "Nope. Gotta get home and call over some random guy so he can take advantage of me. Lots of hair pulling and biting. Maybe tie me up. Use me and abuse me." I smile and turn, knowing his wee wee is shooting through his pants. If he wants to call me a hussy, telling me I let guys take advantage of me, then so be it. I'm gonna make sure he regrets not being the one to do so.

I'm back inside, this time more careful not to slip on the rug. I really need to get someone in to dry this shit. I grab for my phone and shoot out a text to Daryl that I took care of the neighbor.

I'm struggling with which emotion I should allow to take the stage. Anger is definitely in first place right now. Who does Will even think he is, getting in my business like that?

But then there's shock, joy, and surprise at how he tried to avenge my honor. He doesn't even like me, but felt it's his duty to make sure I was being treated with respect? Little did he know if he attempted anything close to those things Stake with Novahope was doing I'd be all over it.

There is no denying all the built-up tension inside me. I've always secretly had a thing for my crazy neighbor. Mind the mouth, I've always been attracted to him. I blamed it on the fact I wasn't getting any, so my brain and vagina were probably starting to panic and take anything they could get. Therefore, whenever the neighbor would come over complaining about something, I'd just tune him out and pretend he was saying other things to me.

It would start out like, "Stay off my yard or else..."

But then my mind would go dark and all I heard was, "Or else I'm gonna take that tight little ass of yours and make it mine, spank you raw until you're begging for my cock to be in you."

Yeah, I know. I really need to get some.

Maybe Daryl was right. I need to get the app, swipe right, and have some random sex. It's that or end up doing my angry neighbor. And I'm not sure that's the answer. He'd probably file harassment charges on me before I got halfway across his lawn and I'd finally be packing my bags.

I refuse to let him win.

Even if my vagina thinks a little neighborly finger bang would really be a nice truce.

I decide to hold off on waving my white flag. My sexual needs aren't in danger of being extinct at this time.

Just as I decide to head to the bedroom and take care of my horniness myself, a knock on my front door sounds. I peek out the window, knowing if it's Will, I'm going to run and grab my shaving cream. Instead, I see a cute, young fireman. Which reminds me… *That jerk*! I look out my side window to see Will still standing on his porch. He seems to have put some pants on, thank God. Someone needs to call the HOA on *him* and that big ol' thing he's scaring small children with.

"Coming!" I shout as I run to my room and grab my pink silk robe and a set of handcuffs in my nightstand from an old Halloween costume.

Then, I answer the door.

"Hello, Miss Hamilton?" the cute fireman addresses me.

I smile like the polite little innocent girl I am. With my voice as low as can be, I say, "Okay, listen, this is what's gonna happen. I'm gonna say a few things I don't really mean, and then I'm gonna jump on you. You need to just simply not drop me and walk me into my house. Got it?"

His eyes go wide as saucers. "Excuse me?"

I don't give him time to tell me no. I start to yell, "Thank God you came. I'm super horny and really need someone to fuck me into tomorrow. Use these on me too." I jump on the guy, who looks horrified. Thankfully, Will can't see his face by the angles of our porches.

He catches me as instructed and I dangle the handcuffs behind his head. "Have your way with me, Mr. Fireman!" I then whisper in his ear, "Okay, you can walk us inside now."

Just before we're out of sight, I turn to the house next door and shout. "I'm so glad to have such a concerned neighbor! My aching vagina thanks you for the call!"

And inside we go.

"Full house," Hank, aka Mr. Fireman says, laying his cards on the table.

"Dammit! How are you so good at this!?" He's beaten me four times in a row. I drop mine and stand. "Want another virgin Manhattan?"

"No thanks, Lil. I should probably get going."

I look at the time. I've kept him kidnapped in my house for almost three hours. I bribed him to stay the rest of the afternoon, but he told me the chief would start to wonder why he never showed back up at work. After walking inside, I had him drop me and apologized for my childish behavior. I confessed that my intentions were solely based on making my neighbor jealous. Then I tried to talk myself out of what I'd just confessed. Was I *trying* to make Will jealous? I just wanted to show him he had no claim on me. But did he? My cobwebbed vagina wanted him to. And why did I want him to validate what he thought of me?

I wasn't really a hussy who allowed people to touch me without my consent. It was my job to flirt with clients. I was a head DJ for WXOJ, Morristown's most popular radio station. We had bands come in and do live shows all the time. We took them out and it was our job to make them happy. Did I get the occasional ass grab and proposition? Sure! Did I ever take anyone up on it? Never. I had lines too. And I never crossed those. It also helped I was never without Daryl, who was a whopping three-hundred fifteen pounds. I had a built-in bodyguard everywhere I went.

Either way, Hank got me to start babbling about all my troubles regarding my neighbor. When I was done, he had checked all the detectors, confirmed they worked, and come to the conclusion that I, in fact, wanted to be with my neighbor.

He was high.

Or maybe I was.

Wanting someone and wanting to *be* with someone were two totally different things. Sex, yes. Dinner dates and sharing a straight edge ruler while we cut his grass perfectly together? No. I told him he didn't like me and the only pussy he'd probably ever get was that damn cat he had. We both got a good laugh out of that and then spent the next two hours playing cards. I served us up some lunch, then once it hit one in the afternoon I made us some drinks. Him a non-alcoholic, of course, because he was on duty.

But it was getting late and I couldn't keep him holed up in my house forever.

"Do you think he's stewing over there, thinking we've

been having animal sex for the past three hours?" I ask, pouring a shot of whiskey, followed by a dash of sweet vermouth.

"I'm not sure. I think all the yelling and moaning you did out your window was a good touch. You don't think he's gonna call my boss, though, do you?"

I offer him a *pfft* sound and say, "No way." When in fact I should be saying, "Probably, sorry. Do they offer a nice severance at your work?"

Hank leaves and limps just as instructed when walking down my porch. Will is nowhere in sight, which sucks because Hank really did play the part. He almost fell down the stairs moaning how sore he was.

To no avail, I go back inside and enjoy the rest of my day off. Come dinner, I look at the time and like clockwork, I hear the dragging of garbage bins being hauled down the driveway next door. This also reminds me that tomorrow is garbage day. And every garbage day, the neighbor throws a hissy fit because I put a measly few bags in his bins. I'm not even sure why he cares. I don't ever have enough garbage to haul those oversized bins to the curb. Not to mention, I'm tiny and they weigh more than I do. It's also not my fault the neighborhood has raccoons that insist on always pushing his trash over and tearing through my bags. Or his bags. Technically they're his since they're in *his* bins.

The more I drink, the more I realize how much Wonka, the tight-ass neighbor, calls and complains on me. Didn't his mommy and daddy teach him that tattling was wrong? That's like kindergarten 101 stuff!

When it strikes close to midnight and I've started seeing double, I grab all my empty bottles and head out my front door super ninja style. Since I'm incredibly sly when I'm totally canned, I line up the bottles right in front of his bins, creating a cute shape, and run back inside my house giggling like a school girl.

I set my alarm for earlier than I need to be up so I can call Waste Management and make a complaint on my messy neighbor who doesn't know how to properly recycle.

Chapter Five

Will

Fridays are for Fines from the City

H e wasn't even that good-looking, for fuck's sake. Receding hairline. Slight gut. Goddamn high-water pants.

And yet…she climbed him like a tree.

I'd been laughing my ass off the moment the fireman showed up to check on her smoke alarms, but things went sour quickly when she invited him in. For. Three. Hours. I swear I wore a hole in my floors pacing in front of the window that looks out to her house.

While they had sex.

Wild, intense, passionate sex.

The thought infuriates me and I don't know why. I don't even like Lilith Hamilton. She's a nuisance and obnoxious.

But the other night?

That dress?

And yesterday morning…those panties.

Fuck. Me.

My dick has no beef with the sexy demon. My dick thinks they can be best friends. My dick wants to take over and start calling the shots.

With Lilith on my mind, I step out of the shower and

towel off. Her pouty red lips. Big brown eyes. Soft, silky hair. Perfect tits. My cock is erect and aching for attention. Not from my hand, no. My cock wants her.

I think I want her too.

Ignoring my dick and those dangerous thoughts, I pull on some boxers and my work slacks. I'm just hunting for an undershirt to wear when the doorbell rings. It's still early, around seven, so I'm confused at who could be stopping by.

Her.

My dick strains against my slacks.

Björk meows at my feet and I nod at my cat. "I know. She's making me crazy. Disrupting my entire damn life." She meows again as if to agree.

And she *is* disrupting my life. I missed my first day of work. Ever. Called in sick. Lied to my supervisor. I wasn't sick, I was a stalker. I just had to know if she was really fucking that fireman. After a few hours, he staggered out of there looking like he'd been put through the wringer. Jealousy was like acid in my veins burning through me.

It's a fact I can no longer deny. As much as I hate Lilith, I need to fuck her. I need to stick my dick inside her and choke her dainty neck until she screams my name.

I'm still in a daze with thoughts of her naked tits jiggling as I plow into her when I answer the door. Instead of seeing my favorite girl to hate, I see an irritated trash man on my front porch. His nametag reads Fred.

"Yeah, so we're going to have to ask you to take care of your little problem. It's against city policy to pick up anything offensive."

I frown at him. "Pardon?"

He throws back a meaty arm and gestures to my trash bin. "The recycling items are to be kept in the recycling bin beside the trash bin. Not all over the street. Furthermore, the offensive shape has required us to write you a citation for two hundred dollars."

"Offensive shape? Two hundred dollars?" I gape at him. "What are you talking about, man?"

He grunts. "Look, if it wasn't you, then it was probably some teenagers. Regardless, we have to cite the homeowner. Sorry, man, but here's your fine." He hands me a pink slip and then waddles down my steps.

Storming after him, I pass his slow ass and make my way to the street. Bottles. Tons of them. In. The. Shape. Of. A. Penis.

Fucking Lilith.

I've just showered and haven't even had time to properly put a shirt on and yet here I am picking up empty liquor and beer bottles. I toss them all into the recycling bin while Fred waits not-so-patiently.

"Thank you and have a nice day," he mutters, his voice monotone the moment I drop the last one inside.

I ignore him and make my way next door, shoving my citation in my pocket.

Bangbangbangbangbang!
Bangbangbangbangbang!
Bangbangbangbangbang!
Bangbangbangbangbang!
Bangbangbangbangbang!
Bangbangbangbangbang!

She cackles with laughter from the other side of the door and it does my head in.

"Open the damn door, woman," I roar, my body physically shaking with fury.

"Oh, hell no. You can stay right outside where you

belong. The last time I let you in, you soaked my house," she gripes.

Rolling my eyes, I squat and lift her silly garden gnome on her porch. Underneath is a key I see her keep there for her big-boy friend. I pluck the key out, push it into the lock, and let myself in.

She squeals when I rush inside. I take a quick note of her outfit. This morning she's wearing tight jeans and a fitted white tank top. I can see the red from her bra underneath and like a bull, I charge for her. I'm not sure what I'll do when I get her in my grip, but I'm going to do something.

"Get out!" she yells as she tries to climb over the back of her couch to escape me.

I clamber over the piece of furniture after her easily and back her into a corner. She holds her palms up to me.

"Truce! I call truce!"

I pounce on her and grab hold of her wrists. My body, against my better judgment, presses to hers and I pin her arms to the wall behind her. With her this close, I can smell her sweet, fruity scent. I want to lick her to see if she tastes good too.

"You can't call truce," I growl.

My cock is hard between us and it takes everything in me not to rut against her. Her brown eyes are no longer wide and worried, they're hooded. From this close, I can see a smattering of cute freckles across her nose and cheeks. She doesn't have any makeup on yet this morning, but she's still so fucking pretty.

"And you can't sit here and hold me against the wall all day just because you're pissed," she taunts, her nostrils flaring.

My gaze falls to her mouth. Fuck, I want to taste her. I

collect both her dainty wrists in one of my hands and free up my other. My fingers brush along her jaw and then I grip her face. I could just pull her jaw down and kiss her sassy mouth.

"I can and I will," I lie. Technically I need to be at work in less than half an hour, but I'm not telling her that. I'll let her sweat it out.

She licks her lips. "Go away, Bottle Boy."

I glower at her. "You have a trash can. Use it."

Her body wriggles against mine, maddening me further. "You fucked the fireman," I spit out bitterly.

She blinks at me in shock. "Yeah, so? Why do you care?"

Because you're mine.

Fuck.

Thank God I don't let that slip.

She's not mine. She can fuck the fireman or Fred or Stake-the-stupid-emo-fucker. I don't care.

"He's probably got a wife and three kids," I sneer.

Hurt flashes in her eyes. "You think I'd fuck some married man?"

"No," I concede with a huff, "but you could at least throw your shit in the married man next door's trash can. Why does it always have to be mine?"

Her lips quirk up on one side in amusement. "Why can't you ever call and bitch about Mr. Paulson, your other neighbor, and his dog that likes to shit in everyone's yards? Why do you always pick on me?" She's being playful, not actually upset. I think she likes it when she has my undivided attention.

I push my glasses up my nose and slide my palm to her hip. Her mouth parts and for a moment, neither of us has anything to say.

"Because you like me, Wonka," she taunts. "Admit you annoy the hell out of me because you like—"

I stop whatever it was that was going to come out of her mouth by pressing my lips to hers. She's frozen for a moment, but when I spear my tongue into her mouth, she lets out a moan that drives the animal inside of me fucking wild. Releasing her wrists, I tangle my hand in her silky hair as I kiss her hard. Furious and punishing. I suck on her tongue and then bite her. She whimpers but pushes her fat tits against my bare chest, desperate for more.

She, my little next door neighbor from hell, tastes like heaven.

My hand slides up beneath the fabric of her tank along the side of her ribs. She's breathing heavy and I can't stop kissing her perfect goddamned mouth. We're headed down a path we can't come back from with my hand inching higher toward her tits when her home phone starts ringing.

"Don't stop," she breathes.

I can't stop. I'm seconds away from tearing off her clothes and fucking her against her wall. I nip at her tongue until a loud, high-pitched voice comes on the answering machine.

"Lilith? Lilith, honey, are you there?"

She freezes in my grip, all heat evaporating from her. "Shit."

"Your father says it's this weekend *or else*. Lance misses you. I know he'd propose if you just gave him three seconds of your time. Bring your tennis racket. We haven't played in ages, darling."

Who the fuck is Lance?

She pushes me away. "Party's over! Gotta go!"

I frown at her sudden change of personality. It's then I

let it sink in what we'd just been doing—what would have happened if we weren't interrupted.

I can't fuck Lilith Hamilton. I barely even like her.

Lies.

The woman on the recorder, whom I assume is her mother, babbles on and on. Lilith goes from being a bubbly seductress to tense and stressed. I want to ask her about it, but she's pushing me out the door.

"Keep your abs on *your* property," she bites out as she pushes me onto the porch. "Keep Big Willy over there too." She gestures at my very obvious erection in my slacks. "Adios, Wonka."

I stewed all day at work over the kiss that almost led to so much more. She's making me lose my mind. I even made an error on a calculation and damn near accused the head of the mortgage department of fraud. What an ass I felt like when I reran the numbers only to conclude I was, in fact, wrong.

I'm *never* wrong.

I yank off my T-shirt and wipe the sweat from my face as I run. My phone is playing some old-school Metallica. The loud, raging guitars not only make me want to pull out my own guitar and start plucking away on some songs, but it also helps pump me up into realizing this morning was a mistake.

Lilith is hot, no doubt.

But I can't stand her.

How does one want to fuck someone they hate?

I'm just rounding the corner to my street when I nearly

trip over my own feet and fall. Lilith, in a black bikini top and a pair of cut-off daisy duke shorts, is washing her cherry-red Mustang in her driveway. The sun is going down, but the sunlight seems to seek her out. Golden strands in her hair catch the light and glimmer. I trot to a stop just to stare.

Fuck, there goes my resolve.

Wet. Bangin' body. Tits and curves and that ass.

I'm hopeless.

I catch the old man, Mr. Daniels, across the street swinging in his porch swing, a goofy grin on his gray-whiskered face. It makes me want to build a fence in front of her house so he can't look at her. Being President of the HOA, I could probably even get away with it…

"Yo, Wonka," she calls out as I near. "You're looking hot."

I puff out my bare chest and smirk because at least someone notices all the hard work—

All thoughts are dashed when cold water blasts me in the face.

"Better cool you off!" she yells as she sprays me down.

She shoots my glasses right off my face and I end up dropping my shirt. I don't stop to pick my shit up but instead chase down the blur who is now running from me while trying to soak me at the same time. I hook an arm around her wet waist but end up stumbling over my own feet since I can't see where the fuck I'm going. We land in her grass with a collective "oomph." She's face down and my dick is conveniently pressed against her ass.

"You live to antagonize me," I grumble as I bury my nose in her hair and inhale her.

She wiggles and the only thing she's successful at doing is making me impossibly harder. "You started it."

"And I'll finish it."

I tug at the string on her neck and then the one at her mid back. With a quick pull, I relieve her of her bikini top.

"Oh no, you just didn't!" she squeals, a loud, adorable laugh escaping from her.

It's then as I rise to my feet with her top in my hand that I realize my crazy neighbor is getting under my skin. She's burying herself deep inside of me so I can't think or focus on anything else. And I'm not sure I want to anyway.

She stands with her palms covering her perfect tits. Her smile is wicked as she arches a brow at me and backs up toward her house. "It's on, Wonka. It's fucking on."

I smirk at her cute, dirty mouth. "Technically it's *off*, demon girl." I sling her top over my shoulder and walk over to collect my glasses and shirt. "Just face it, you're not winning anything." I slide on my glasses so I can fully appreciate the swells of her tits barely contained by her tiny hands.

Her back hits the front door and she shrugs. "We'll see."

And then she flips me off before slipping inside her house.

But not before me and Mr. Daniels get a nice, quick peek of a perfect tit I'm convinced I won't see the last of.

Game on, Lilith, game on.

Chapter Six

Lilith

Saturdays are for Swiping Right

N*o, no, no…*

"Dude, none of these guys look legit. And *this* guy looks like a total serial killer!"

We're sitting in my kitchen and I'm swiping through the Tinder app Daryl finally convinced me to download. After yesterday's mishap, I realized just how desperately I needed some action. Daryl and I hope I'll find a solid guy to work out all my frustration with before I make a judgement error and have super spontaneous sex with Wonka.

"Girl, you've passed like twenty guys in a matter of three seconds. You're being too damn picky." He tries to snatch up my phone, but I pull away.

"How is making sure my lady parts don't get murdered or get the clap being too picky?"

Daryl sighs, sitting back on the island bar stool. "Just pick one. If he ain't who he says he is, I'll scare him off."

At that, I laugh. "What? You gonna stick around just to make sure he gets me off too?"

Daryl looks like I just gave him cooties. "Ew, girl, you're like my sister. I don't wanna hear you moan and groan on that dick. Just saying if he ain't who he says he is, I'd be here to tell him to get gone."

As much as that sounds like a good idea, something else comes to mind. "I actually have a better idea." I go into the app. There were a few who weren't so bad-looking. Jerald, thirty-five, looks to be eight miles away. His tagline says, *I hope you have a big trunk because I'm gonna put my bike in it.* Not sure where that bike is really going but screw it. I swipe right. "Shit, here we go—"

An instant ding chimes back telling me good ol' Jerald, swiped right back. "Geez, that was fast."

We're both leaning into my phone, waiting for something to happen. "So, what happens now?"

Another ding, notifying me I have a message.

"This dude is eager to get on it." Daryl laughs, leaning closer, so we can both read the message.

Jerald: Sup hot stuff. Glad u like what u see. Hope ur hungry. Want me to cum to u? Daddy gonna fill u up.

"What in God's name?" I ask, shocked, while Daryl's rolling off his chair laughing.

"What exactly is he going to fill me up with?" I'm confused. I turn to Daryl, who's holding his chest laughing hysterically. I smack him on the shoulder. "I'm for real. What's he talking about?"

"Girl, don't worry, just tell him you're hungry and come on over." He chuckles and I just shrug my shoulders and reply.

Me: Great. Can't wait. Come to my place.

I quickly punch in the address.

"Ain't that your neighbor's house number, Lil?"

"Sure is, D. That way if he shows up and he's not who he says he is, we don't have to worry. We stay inside and let the neighbor shoo him off. If he is, then I simply pop out my front door and silly ol' me will tell him I must have typed in the wrong address. Blame it on how famished I am."

Daryl starts to laugh again as I click send.

"Now we wait."

Daryl makes himself comfortable on the couch while I go and find something sexy to wear. I put on a red lace bra and panties and throw on my cream silk robe. Since Jerald is only eight miles away I know I have limited time to prep.

"A car's pullin' up!" Daryl shouts and I come running down the hallway. We both dart to the side window, which gives us a perfect view of the neighbor's front porch.

"Oh shit, he's getting out... *Oh shit,* is he wearing *leggings*?"

"Damn, is he wearing a chick's top?"

We're both staring out the window, our eyes popped as we watch a suped-up version of Lance Armstrong walk up Will's porch steps.

"I guess the bike comment makes sense now," I say, and Daryl gives me a get a clue look. "What? He obviously rides bikes."

"Honey, you need to get out more."

Whatever. I look back next door and—

"Whoa" and "What the?" come flying out of our mouths at once.

"Dude, where's his dick?"

I'm wondering the same thing.

"Does he have that shit tucked back?" Daryl asks, pressing his face closer to the window.

"Hell if I know!"

We watch as Jerald walks up to the door and knocks.

"Okay. What're you gonna do? Not sure this is the guy. I mean, he tucked his shit. Who tucks their dick and balls?"

Again, how the hell should I know? I'm not a dude. Maybe it's a biker thing. Okay, maybe not. "Hard pass," I say and shake my head. I'm not even fully convinced that's a dude.

A few seconds pass, and the door opens. Will steps out, looking confused as to why there's a she-dude on his porch. We can't see what words are being exchanged, but I'm pretty sure it's something like,

Jerald: "Hi, I'm looking for Candy. She swiped right and now I'm gonna put my bike in her."

Wonka: "There's no Candy here, but your car is leaking oil onto my driveway. Get off my property before I call the cops, my HOA buddies, and the mayor."

Jerald: "Got it. Any chance you'd be inter—"

"He's leaving. Your neighbor doesn't look happy."

Wah, wah. When does he? *Oh, I don't know. He looked pretty content when his tongue was down your throat yesterday.* I can actually still taste the mint and coffee off his tongue.

Eventually, we remove ourselves from the window. We take a seat on the couch and grab for my phone. "Okay, that was a bust," I say, opening the app. I go through another round of pics until I find another decent one.

"Okay, how about Biff?"

"His name is Biff? What is this, *Back to the Future*?" Daryl laughs, shaking his head and forcing me to pass on poor Biff.

"Fine, what about this one?" I stop on Phil. Not the sexiest name, but his profile pic is kinda hot. "He's younger than me. But that can be a good thing, right?" Not that it's by much. It says he's twenty-five, but age is only a number. His tagline reads, *I might be young, but I need you to help me grow,* with a fancy picture made of letters and symbols. "Wait, is that supposed to be a—"

A dick. He made a dick using letters and symbols. Wow.

"He's entrusting you to make his dick grow, yes."

Shit. That was creative.

I decide to give him a shot. I approve of his picture talent. I swipe right.

This one takes a few minutes longer to reply. I get up and grab some beers while Daryl uses the bathroom. It's after I'm forced to open a few windows because he bombed out my toilet that we hear the ding.

"We're in!" I yell as Daryl makes his way back to the living room. I type in the same message, wanting him to come to my place, and offer up Wonka's address. Phil was fifteen miles away but responds that he's actually right around the corner. Only a few minutes pass until we're back up at the window and see a car pull up in front of his house.

"Oh, hell no."

"Is this *really* happening?" I ask in amazement as we both witness *Phil*, looking closer to nineteen, get out of what looks like it could be his mother's car.

"Dude, is that his mom dropping him off for a booty call?" Just then we hear him yell back to the car. "Thanks, Mom. Pick me up in an hour."

"Oh, *hell* no! Girl, another pass."

"Well, no fucking shit! I'm not a creep!" I mean, I don't think I am. The kid is still kinda cute. Sandy blond hair and tall. He's wearing glasses, but for some reason those particular ones just don't do it for me. He's wearing a pair of skinny jeans and a—

"Is that Justin Bieber on his shirt?" I can't even with this. I bust out laughing.

Daryl joins in as we watch reject number two bang on Wonka's door. Same as before, Will answers, stepping outside onto his porch looking pissed. As their lips move, I'm hearing:

Wonka: "Whatever it is you're selling I'm not buying it. Are you registered with the city to be selling door to door?"

Bieber/Phil: "Bro, I'm here for Candy? I only have an hour so..."

Wonka: "There is no Candy here."

Bieber/Phil: "Nah, bro. I want to do Candy, not eat it. Well, maybe eat her—"

"Damn yo, your neighbor's brutal. Poor kid just went running. I wonder what the hell he said to him."

"No idea," I say and pull away from the window. I crack open a fresh beer and toss myself back onto the couch. Well, this isn't going as planned. "I thought you said this app was legit?" I take a swig of my beer. Maybe it's a sign. I'm not meant to have random sex. I need to do it the old-fashioned way and go to church. That's where all the good men are.

"You have some strange-ass luck." Daryl pops open his beer and falls onto the seat next to me.

"Well, what do we do now?"

He shrugs. "I guess we keep at it until we find the one."

Five beers later and another three failed swipe attempts, we're sitting on my couch in tears at the latest failed swipe. "Oh my God. Did you even see him? I swear he was wearing makeup," I snort, taking a sip of my drink.

"You two could share fashion tips," Daryl says, holding his chest.

"I don't know, I really think I should have said yes to

Freedom, though. I mean, who names their kid *Freedom*?"

Daryl almost spits out his sip. "The dude's tagline said, *'I need you to free-dom nuts.'* What did you expect?"

I barrel over, the tears falling down my cheeks I'm laughing so hard. I'm concentrating so hard on not peeing my pants, when my front door flies open. I lift to see Will storming into my house.

Shit!

"Uh, yeah…normal people knock." I get up, my cheeks flaming red to match his anger. Yep, he doesn't look happy. "Geez, Willy, having a bad day?" I try and play it off, but I have a small itch that tells me he may have caught on.

He's up in my face and I can't help but inhale the scent of him. I can tell he's freshly showered by the aroma of soap and cologne seeping into my nostrils.

"You having fun over here, Lilith? Or should I call you *Candy*?"

Yep, gig's up. Doesn't mean *I* should give up, though. "I'm not sure what you're talking about. I never pegged you for one to role play—"

He cuts my banter short, grabbing my waist and pulling my body into his. The air expels from my lungs at the way he feels pressed against me. The humor in me dies as I stare into his angry blue eyes. God, he's hot. Even more so when he's mad. Not that I've ever seen him *not* mad. His jaw is tight, but it only accentuates his sharp cheekbones and his perfect, sexy nose. His skin is tanned and smooth. There's no doubt he takes care of himself. I make a mental note to ask about his daily regiment, when his grip on me tightens. His head lowers and I swear he's about to kiss me. *Do it… do it. Oh God, kiss me again.* He might be a bad idea, but hot damn does this man know how to kiss. And ever since the first time, the memory hasn't left my mind. I may or may not have done a little bit of masturbating to the thought.

He lowers his head and my eyes close. My lips part as I await his mouth on mine. But it never comes. He passes my mouth, leaning past me, and snags my phone out of my robe pocket.

"Hey! That's mine!" I bark, trying to get it back, but he's making it impossible to grab with his long arm holding me away. "Dude, Wonka, you can't just take my phone!"

He ignores me.

Right about now I wish I had a lock on my phone. I hated always having to remember the passcode at night after a few too many. The countless amount of times I locked myself out, so I disabled the feature. "Will, seriously…"

Shit, what's he doing?

He's tapping away on my phone. Typing, swiping, typing some more. I turn to Daryl, who's no help since he's got a pillow over his face laughing. So much for that bodyguard.

Finally, he tosses my phone back, and I barely catch it.

"What did you just do?" I look down and see the Tinder app open.

"At least when using my address, send over my type." Then he turns and storms out.

I look down and see he's swiped a bunch of girls *and* given them his address.

"He did not!" I turn back to Daryl in complete shock at what my jerkhole neighbor just pulled. "Can you believe him?"

"Girl, you two need to just bang already."

What I need to do is take a bat and bang him in the head with it! I can't believe he used *my* Tinder account to get laid!

And not just laid by one. But by three tramps! He swiped himself three ugly girls, mind you. And in the past hour I've watched all three show up and NOT leave. What in God's name is that guy doing over there? There's no way he's banging them all. He's too anal to have a foursome. I mentally laugh at my jab, but then I hear giggling. I run to the window and watch all three women walk out, smiles from ear to ear on their ugly-ass faces.

That jerk.

What a sleazeball.

"That's it."

"What's it?" Daryl asks, pulling his attention away from the TV.

"I'm going over there and giving him a piece of my mind." I storm over to the door.

"In your lingerie collection? You may want to put some clothes on before doing that unless you want to become number four on his list for the day."

I pick up a gym shoe and throw it at him. He ducks, but not before letting out a howl of laughter.

"He's already seen this." Which is true.

I storm out and across his lawn. I make sure to smash my feet into the grass, knowing I'm damaging his precious lawn. When I get up to his front porch, I raise my hand to bang like hell on his door.

Before my fist has the chance to make contact, the door flies open. A large hand grabs mine and yanks me inside.

Chapter Seven
Will

Saturdays are for All Nine Inches

What the fuck is she even wearing?

I glower at her as I take in her appearance. Red. I see red. Hidden behind a sheer robe of some sorts. Bra and matching panties. Definitely not something she should be strutting around the neighborhood in for all to see.

"Let go of me, skank," she yells at me, her cheeks blazing red with fury.

Skank?

I flash her a smug grin. "Oh, *them.*"

She tries to pull her arm free, but I don't let her go. Fuck, I don't know if I can *ever* let her go. Not when she feels so right in my grip.

"Yeah, them," she practically growls. "I know you aren't into orgies, Willy, so tell me what you were doing with all those hussies!"

"How do you know I'm not into orgies?"

She blinks and gapes at me. "You had sex with all three of them?"

I pull her to me until her body is flush against mine. Her head tilts up so she can regard me, her brown eyes glimmering with accusation. She's jealous. Sexy, rotten, evil little Lilith is jealous.

"I had to teach them a lesson," I say with a smirk.

Her eyes narrow. "What sort of lesson?"

My palm slides down her back and I settle it on her toned ass. "The important kind."

She bites on her bottom lip and fuck all if I don't want to bite on it too. My cock aches between us.

"Did you spank them?"

I arch a brow. "No, but I threatened to. Mitzy was a mess. I really wanted to set her straight."

She lets out a frustrated sound and tries to push away. I hold her tighter against me with my hand firmly gripping her ass.

"And Bailey?" I shake my head. "I'll be seeing her again soon because she needs a lot more work."

"I hate you," she breathes.

I reach between us and tug at the silky belt that holds her robe together. It comes loose and her breath hitches.

"But Lylah was the worst. I could work on her every day for weeks and she'd still be so—"

"Enough!" she screeches. "I don't want to hear about your conquests. You're a pig, Wonka."

I'm amused at how pissed she is. It makes me want to provoke her some more. Payback's a bitch.

"You try to fight dirty, but I don't lose, demon." I lean forward and breathe against her ear. "Never."

She lets out a sigh when I slide the silky material of her robe off her shoulders. I want to see what she has hiding underneath. Lilith has a killer body and I'm not immune to it.

"Why did you send them to my house?" I ask as the robe falls to the floor.

"I was looking for someone to fuck me," she taunts, a wicked gleam in her eyes.

Her words hit their intended mark because I'm instantly furious. "You were going to fuck one of those freaks?"

She rolls her eyes and I pop her ass, making her squeak. "No, Wonka, I wasn't going to fuck one because they were all creeps. I wanted to separate the good from the bad by sending them over here." She smirks. "Unlucky for you, they were all bad."

"All I heard was blah blah blah you were going to fuck one if they were hot. Are you kidding me right now, Lilith? That was dangerous. You're going to get yourself killed one day!" I snap.

She squirms in my arms but frees her hand so she can pop me upside the head. "Still, none of your business."

I slap her ass hard and she yelps. *"You,"* I hiss, "are my business."

"If you cared so much, you wouldn't have been getting freaky with all those kinky Tinder twats! You're such an ass—"

Gripping her jaw, I stare down at her. "I balanced their checkbooks."

"Ohhh, so that's what we're calling it nowadays," she mocks. Then her voice turns deep as she imitates me. "I'll add a seven right here." Her hips thrust, rubbing against my erection.

"You know I'd add a *lot* more than a seven. Try a nine, baby."

She snorts. "Why don't you subtract one, Wonka? You may be Big Willy, but you ain't that big!"

Lifting her by her curvy ass, I walk her over to the nearest wall. Her legs wrap around my waist just as I grind against her center. "Do you feel that?" I growl. "Do we need to count the inches? Do I need to call Mitzy, Bailey, and Lylah over here to measure it for us?"

"Asshole," she breathes but rolls her head to the side, offering me her sweet neck.

I run my tongue along the side of her neck until I'm at her earlobe. I bite it and then whisper, "Just admit you're wrong. Besides, I'm the only man who's allowed to touch this." I rub against her in just the right way that has her moaning.

"Maybe I wanted the dick-tucking Lance Armstrong to tuck his penis inside my—"

I silence her taunt with my mouth. Kissing her is too easy. She's a bad girl who makes me crazy but kissing her is unlike anything I've ever felt. Maddening and exhilarating all at once. Her fingers find my hair and she tugs while she kisses me back just as hard. Our tongues are at war, but our bodies are desperate to connect.

"Will," she moans against my lips. "I want…"

I hold her with one arm as I push my sweatpants down my thighs. "I know," I murmur. "All nine inches."

She laughs but when I pull her pretty red panties to the side, she lets out a sharp breath of air. I tease her opening with my tip and then push all the way into her slick cunt before either of us has a chance to rethink our actions.

Fuck, she's tight.

"Oh my God," she whines, her fingers yanking at my hair.

I find her mouth again with mine and dominate hers. My hips thrust against her and pleasure zings up my spine. This girl feels too damn good.

"Will," she murmurs. "What are we doing?"

"We're fucking, baby," I growl and then tug at her bottom lip with my teeth.

Sliding my palm between us, I seek out her clit. As soon as I touch her there, her cunt clenches around my cock. I need to get her off quickly or I'm going to come like a loser after only a few moments of being inside her. Slowing my thrusting, I focus on bringing her to an orgasm. Her breathing is ragged and she keeps whimpering. With every passing second, she gets closer and closer.

"You're going to delete that app," I bark, my teeth nipping at her jaw.

She starts shaking as her climax nears. "And you're going to stop balancing skanks' checkbooks."

I laugh as I slam into her hard enough to knock a picture from the wall. It crashes to the floor, but I'm so wild for her, I don't have it in me to worry about the mess right now.

"Tax returns too," she moans. "I know what a sneaky nerd you are."

A growl rumbles through me as I suck on her dainty neck. Her cunt clenches because my sweet neighbor from hell loves it. Well, I fucking love it too. I suck and suck, leaving marks all over her perfect skin as I fuck her into tomorrow. And just when my arm begins to ache from holding her up while I pound her like a nail into the wall, she loses it. Her body jolts and shudders, her pussy clenching so hard around me I nearly black out. My cock jerks as I spurt out my orgasm and I quickly pull out, the rest of my cum shooting on her belly between us and then sliding back down as gravity takes over.

I slowly set her to her feet, but my hand doesn't want to leave her ass. Ever.

"I think you should stay over tonight," I murmur, my

lips brushing against hers.

She shakes her head. "I can't. I have to go see my parents in the morning."

"Then come over after," I demand. "I'm not done with you."

I'm not sure I'll ever be.

She pushes me away and puts her hands on her hips. In her sexy red lingerie and my dripping cum painted all over her stomach, I'm about three seconds from not giving her a choice. I'd love to restrain my little demon in my bed.

"You've got an evil look in your eyes, Wonka. Like that time I accidentally egged your house." She sticks her tongue out at me and then leaps past the broken glass from the frame.

"You can't accidentally egg someone's house, Lilith." That shit really pissed me off.

She shrugs as she picks up her robe and slides it back on, my cum soaking the material. "Just sayin' you're all kinds of evil tonight."

I take a step toward her and she backs up to the door. "Grandma will be here tomorrow for dinner," I tell her. "You should come eat with us." My grandmother will have a shit fit if she finds out we're together. And even though Lilith is trying to hightail it out of here like her pants are on fire, we *are* together. She started it and I'll finish it. With her in my bed all night where I can punish her sweet ass for an entire year for all the torment she's caused me.

"Evil," she says with a laugh. "Bye, Willy."

She slips out and the door clicks closed behind her.

This. Fucking. Girl.

I grin because she's doing my head in, *again*, and I like it.

I've officially lost my mind over Lilith Hamilton.

And I'm not sure I want it back.

I clean up the broken frame and pace my house. I let her go. She's been gone all of five minutes and I already miss her. Crazy-ass Lilith who's been testing the limits of my sanity for a year now. When did she manage to get to me? I decide to take a long, hot shower to see if my feelings for her disappear with some time passing. But after imagining her naked and in the shower with me, I end up jacking off and it only makes me want her more. I dress in a pair of basketball shorts and throw on a T-shirt before heading to my front porch swing so I can spy on her. I grab my Gibson acoustic guitar on my way out.

I settle in the swing and lazily strum some chords. It's the only part of my past I couldn't let go of. I'm lost in my thoughts—to a time when I was a really shitty human—when I hear voices. Lilith's friend leaves and she waves to him from the porch. I greedily devour her appearance. She's recently showered and put on something a little more normal. Black yoga pants and a pink tank top. Her brown hair is a mess twisted into an unkempt bun that makes her look hot as fuck.

"Keep going," she says from her yard.

I strum my guitar again. "I will if you come sit with me."

She prances across the yard and bounds up my porch steps. I want to maul her the moment she sits, but she seems so eager to hear me play that I refrain. We don't speak—an anomaly in and of itself—and I just strum songs from the nineties.

"'Polly' by Nirvana," she guesses as she leans against my side, resting her head on my shoulder as she yawns. "Easy."

"You know more than Snoop and Dr. Dre?" I deadpan.

She laughs. "I'm full of surprises."

We grow quiet again and I play Pearl Jam's "Better Man."

"I didn't know you played guitar, Wonka."

"I'm full of surprises too."

Song after song I play and I realize this is the calmest I've felt in a long time. Usually, I'm wound so tight and everything agitates me. And now, the one who agitates me the most is giving me peace.

"Lilith?"

Her breathing is soft and rhythmic. She's asleep. I lean over and prop my guitar against the house.

I let out a sigh as I stroke my fingers down the outside of her arm. "I was a bad person," I whisper, knowing she can't hear me. "I was a bad person and this"—I wave around me—"this was supposed to be my way of fixing that. The perfect house. My hard-earned job. Yard of the damn month." I close my eyes and pinch the bridge of my nose, willing those nightmares from my past to go away. "I'm sorry I'm *still* not a good person."

I scoop her into my arms and stand. She stirs slightly as I carry her next door. Once I've laid her on her bed and covered her with a blanket, I run my knuckles along her temple and leave.

I've been such a dick to her.

I was supposed to grow the fuck up and stop being a selfish asshole.

And yet...I've done nothing but continually fuck up when it comes to her.

Chapter Eight

Lilith

Sundays are for Tiaras and Tongue Fucking

"Lilith, dear, sit up straight."

Lilith, dear, sit up straight.

I internally mock my nagging mother and scoot up in my chair, adjusting the tiara I wore to annoy her. When she phoned this morning suggesting what I should wear to brunch, she went on and on about royal weddings. This was her way of making it clear she wanted me in my Stepford wife outfit. The perfect fitting dress that poofs at the end. Nude heels because any other color would be too suggestive for a lady. And curls. Don't forget the perfect girly, shoot me, curls. So, when I showed up in a turtleneck dress and a tiara, almost half an hour late, mind you, it left her with no time to drag me upstairs to my old room and redress me.

I sit straight to please her but push out my breasts for dramatics. She gives me the 'watch your manners' look and I smile back with my sweet, 'yes, Mommy Dearest' look. Maybe if Loser Lance wasn't going on and on about his boring lawyer cases, I wouldn't be falling asleep at the breakfast table.

"Lance, that is absolutely fascinating, isn't it, Lilith?"

Mother says and turns to me just as I shove a large strawberry in my mouth. The look of distress suddenly fills her aging features at my unladylike eating habits.

"Oh, yeah, uh, yuper gweat." I chew down the gigantic bite, juice from the strawberry dripping down my chin. I hear my mother sigh. Good. Maybe she'll finally realize I'm a lost cause and leave me alone.

"Maybe some time I can give you a tour of my office," Lance says as if he's doing me a favor.

Maybe I should just throw myself off the balcony.

I nod, putting another piece of fruit in my mouth, probably causing heart palpitations for my poor mother, and reply, "Yeah, wow. Sounds like the best time ever, but right now I'm really busy at work."

"Lilith," Mother warns me.

"What? I am. The station has a great lineup of bands the next upcoming weeks, and D and I have to write scripts."

My father pulls the newspaper away from his face, closes it, and sets it on the dining room table. "You shouldn't waste your time on that hobby. I'm sure they can find someone else to handle that. Lance, my daughter would love to tour your law firm."

Actually, no, I would not.

And maybe now's a good time to bring up what my father is trying to do with the radio station. This is exactly why I've been avoiding these damn brunches. Because my parents just don't get it. They don't get me. They can't see past the person they've already created in their heads. And in those heads, I'm marrying Loser Lance and spending the remainder of my days planning galas and tea parties alongside my mother.

Lance makes another attempt at conversation with me.

"I've been meaning to tell you, you look lovely this morning," he says, smiling like a stupid buffoon.

I let out an accidental snort.

"Lilith, manners," my mother barks as I cover my mouth, trying to hide my laughter.

Is he serious right now? I want to turn to him and tell him to stop talking. Maybe respond with *thanks, I don't normally wear turtleneck dresses in the middle of summer, but I went to pound town with my neighbor yesterday and he sucked the bejesus out of my neck, leaving tons of love marks. I currently resemble a horny teenage girl who let her nerdy but buff boyfriend suck all over her neck for the fun of it. It was fun, all right...*

Lance's parents and mine have been friends since college. And when they grew older together they made plans. Plans Lance went along with as well. Little does *Lance* know I'm just not into guys with comb-overs and this story does not end with I dos and making mini comb-over, boring lawyer babies.

God, that makes me want to gag just thinking—

"Oh goodness, are you okay? Are you choking on some fruit?" Lance leans over, patting at my back.

Nope, just the scary thought of our future together. "No, all good," I say and take a big sip of my water. The mention of my attire also reminds me of my neighbor. No doubt, Lance mistakes my reddening cheeks as the cause for the embarrassing snort, rather than the real reason. Little does he know it's because my mind is in the gutter thinking about how Wonka and Big Willy pounded me nasty style against his wall last night. It was super-hot. Way hotter than what I imagined when I'd masturbated to the thought of sex with him.

Not that it was often.

It was often.

He was, what they call a man who knows his way around a woman's body. I could easily have blamed it on the fact I hadn't had sex in forever, but the way he handled me... lifting me and shoving me against the wall like a crazed man on a mission. Hot. Hot. Hot.

Will always carries that look on him. The one that says he wishes he knew how to shut me up sometimes. And I think last night he finally figured out how. Then again, I'd cut my own tongue out if I got the orgasm he gave me last night over and over.

"Lilith, you're slouching again."

Yeah, because my body is like jelly thinking about every time my back banged against the wall. I probably can't wear backless shirts for a while until the sex bruises fade.

Lance scoots his chair closer to me and places his hand over mine. He leans in, his voice low. "Don't feel embarrassed. I find snorting very attractive."

Ew! I stare at his unwelcomed hand. Unlike Will, whose masculine hands were made to touch me, Lance's are dainty. And to be really honest, way too fucking hairy. He should look into taking some of his obnoxious finger hair and using it for his premature balding.

I pull my hand from under his and remove my linen napkin from my lap. "Well, this has been so delightful. Mother, Father." I turn, addressing both my parents. "I'd forgotten just how amazing your Sunday brunches are. But I really need to get back home. I have an early day tomorrow."

"Lilith, sit—"

I stand up, ignoring my father's demand. I turn to Lance. "It was nice seeing you again. Good luck in life." My statement confuses him. I find it to be pretty self-explanatory. I turn, giving my back to everyone, and walk out of my parents' breakfast room and hustle through the expansive kitchen where I left my purse.

"Lilith, you get back here this instant."

I don't turn at the voice of my father. I reach the counter and grab my purse and jacket.

"I'm not going to tolerate this behavior from you."

That statement has me glowering at Daddy. "What behavior? That I won't sit there any longer and have you call my job a hobby? Let that poor guy think we have a future? I'm not your puppet, Daddy. I'm not going to let everyone else plan my life."

His eyes are wild with anger. No one talks to Bart Hamilton this way. Not even his daughter. "Your immature plan to go find yourself is over, Lilith. I gave you the year you asked for, even against my better judgement. Your mother convinced me this was just a phase. But I'm done watching you jeopardize your future."

"How am I jeopardizing my future?"

"Watch your tone with me, young lady."

"No! You keep saying this is some phase. That I'm just playing around. I'm doing what I want to be doing—"

"Nonsense. You're working at a dump radio station that is dying."

"It's not dying. Or is that why you're trying to purchase it? So you can kill it yourself?"

"It's not for you. It's a male's position anyway. You should be at home. Taking care of your husband and raising your children."

My mouth falls open.

And there it is.

My father, the sexist asshole.

"You know what, Daddy? I am *not* coming home. I'm staying where I'm at and I'm going to continue to work at the station. Doing what *I* love. You don't own me." I turn around and storm away. But not before hearing the threatening last words of my father.

"You will come home, or I will take everything away from you. Do not test me, Lilith. You know who will win this one. I always do."

A sad part of me knows as well.

Bart Hamilton always wins.

By the time I pull into my driveway, the sun has gone down, and the night sky is as dark as my mood. My father has been making threats to get me home since the day I left. But I've never felt he'd actually go through with them until now. He promised me one year. Exactly what I asked for. I just didn't think once that year was up, he'd still be so adamant. I thought he'd see how much happier I am and want that for his daughter. But today only proves it's not about what I want or making sure I'm happy. It's about him and his image and social status.

Growing up in a family that's wealthy is not all it's cracked up to be. People are envious of the ones who have heavy bank accounts and ritzy, material things. I used to hate how labeled I felt. In school with girlfriends. Any guy I dated. It all fell back to the fact I came from money and lots of it. Girls were mean because they tagged me as the snobby rich girl. Boys used me because they wanted to reap the benefits of a rich girlfriend. It was all fake and I hated it. While people wished they were me, I looked back wishing to be them. I wanted to come home to a simple house and eat meatloaf and talk about my day at school. Crap, I would have loved to come home and play video games and drink soda. Instead, I ate du jour and fancy fish, and God knows what other strange delicacies. I had French lessons, tennis lessons, piano lessons, singing lessons. While everyone else got to be normal kids, I was too busy being molded into a goddamn debutante.

I slam my car door and head up my porch. I notice Will's living room light's on, which means he's home. No way would he waste precious energy and not be there to use it. I make a pit stop at home and grab an aged bottle of twenty-one-year-old Balvenie Scotch.

Walking across the lawn barefoot, I appreciate the feel of the soft grass under my feet. Even though he's anal beyond belief, he sure does have a green thumb. I take his front steps two at a time, and without bothering to knock I test the door handle, find it surprisingly unlocked, and walk in.

Will is sitting on the couch. He's shirtless, in only a pair of running shorts. He's got one hand around a beer and the other—

"Am I interrupting something?" I ask him and his missing hand which is down his pants.

He doesn't panic or look shocked that I walked in on him grabbing his junk. His hand also doesn't move from inside his shorts.

"Yeah, it's called adjusting my balls. You here to do it for me?" He's so damn sexy just sitting there looking all laid back. A side I rarely get to see of him since he's always yelling at me.

"Your door was unlocked, Mr. Neighborhood Watch." I arch a brow at him. "Someone could have just walked in and got you."

He flashes me a wide grin that makes me grow weak in the knees. "Maybe I was waiting for that someone."

God, he's so cute.

From the time it takes me to get from his front door to his couch, a billion different scenarios flow through my head. Everything from sucking him off to falling on the couch and hoping he just hugs me while I cry out all the stress I have building up.

I wish my father would approve of someone like Will. Someone who's stable, hardworking, and kind in an anal-retentive sort of way. But he would never meet Bart Hamilton's expectations.

By the time I make it to the couch, a more stable scenario wins. I uncap the bottle and take a huge swig, allowing the whiskey to burn as it slides down my throat. "I've had a really bad day, Wonka, so I don't need any of your lip. Got it?"

He's looking at me. Assessing me. My skin immediately feels on fire the way his eyes take me in. Like he's devouring me.

"You want to talk about it?" he asks, as I recap the bottle and set it down on an end table.

I grab for his beer bottle, dropping it on the coffee table in front of him. "Talking is the last thing I want to do right now." I climb on top of him, straddling his lap. My hands go up, threading into his hair. It's still damp, which means he's freshly showered. I grip hard, pulling him to me, and press my lips to his. I love the way they feel on mine. The way his muscled thighs feel under me. The way his hands grip my ass, tugging closer.

"God, you smell good. What's your secret?" I moan,

deepening our kiss.

"Men's soap. I thought you didn't want to talk." He sucks my lower lip into his mouth and bites.

"You're right. Stop talking." I grip his hair harder. The low growl in his throat sends waves of pleasure to my core. His hands, once again, are gripping my ass, making me grind against him. "Jesus," I pant as he deepens our kiss. Our tongues are at war. I'm so turned on, I might not make it past the dry humping, which is fine with me.

"What's got my girl all worked up tonight?"

I grind into him, causing us both to moan. "I'm not your girl. Just the neighbor who needs to spend some quality time riding out all the wear and tear of her day."

Will pushes my dress up my thighs, exposing my pink thong. Shoving the thin material to the side, his thick finger begins working at my clit.

"I don't fuck around, Lilith. You want to talk, I'll talk. But if you want this…" He rams one finger inside me.

I moan, throwing my head back.

"Yeah, I think that's what you want. Are you my girl, Lilith?"

"No, I'm no one's girl. But try two fingers. Two can be more persuasive."

The low chuckle off his lips sends me into a tailspin. Dammit, he's so sexy. I wonder why he doesn't laugh more. I'd seriously drop my panties every single time if I were rewarded with that sound.

"What's it going to be, baby?" he murmurs. It's then he rewards me with another finger.

Shit. I start riding his hand.

"If you were *my* girl, I'd give you three fingers. Four if you're good. Take my tongue to your wet pussy and devour you. Fuck you with it until you quiver around my tongue. Then I'd fuck you with my cock."

I'm panting, riding his hand harder, pulling at his hair.

"What's it going to be, Lilith?"

"I'm sooo your girl."

That damn low chuckle, the sound is going to make me come. He sticks to his word and three fingers go in. I can't take any more and I lose it. I start to orgasm.

"That's it, baby, ride it out."

I do. Oh boy, I do. Once I start coming down, he startles me by quickly standing, with me still in his arms. He rotates so my back is to the couch, and without warning, he drops me. My back hits the soft cushion on a squeal. I lift my head, still dizzy, wondering what he's up to. With the darkness in his eyes, I have a feeling I know what's next.

I watch, feeling high on lust, as Will bends down, latching his fingers around my thong string. He tugs them down my legs and tosses them. He crawls back up my legs, his face disappearing in between my thighs. My back arches the second his tongue hits my clit.

"Oh, Jesus," I moan as I fall back, grabbing at anything to hold on to. He starts lapping at me, using one hand to hold my wild hips down and the other to tease my center. He takes no prisoners as he licks and sucks, bites and pulls at my lips until I'm seeing double. He wasn't kidding when he said he was going to devour me. My body is on fire. My skin doesn't feel like my own, it's so sensitive. I want him to stop because I'm going to break, but I need him to keep going. And never ever stop.

"I love fucking you with my mouth," he growls, jabbing his tongue deep inside me.

"Oh God," I hiss. "Who would have thought

you'd ever use your mouth for other things besides complaining—*ahhhh!*"

He bites down, almost causing a blackout.

His hands are spreading me open as he goes to town. I'm like a wild animal under him, thrashing and moaning.

"*Yes, more. Yes…*"

"You like that, baby?" Harder, faster. "Tight and sweet." He shoves three fingers in me while still using his tongue to pleasure my clit. "Mine now. Hear me? Mine."

Why is him saying that turning me on so badly? My toes begin to curl, and I can't fight the blast that's about to shoot through me. My legs start to tighten around his head. I don't want to suffocate him, but when my orgasm erupts, I squeeze so tight, there's no way air is getting to his brain.

"That's it. Come on my tongue. Fuck…"

And just like that, my bossy neighbor gets his way—like always—because I explode, soaking his tongue with my orgasm. When my hips finally fall back onto the couch, I open my eyes to see him wiping at his chin.

"I'm going to fuck you with my cock now," he tells me, a smug grin on his face. "But first, I have to ask. What's with the tiara?"

Chapter Nine

Will

Mondays are for Tinderbites

"Talk to me," I insist as I stroke her hair. My bedroom is dark and we've exhausted ourselves. I should be heading to bed, knowing I have an early day tomorrow, but I have an unusually quiet naked Lilith in my arms.

She stiffens. "I should go home."

"You're not going home tonight, so you may as well spill it. Tell me what's bothering you. Is it us?" I'm not sure what the hell we're doing anymore, but I have no desire to stop it.

"No, Wonka," she says, a smile in her voice. "We're pretty good. My sore vagina can attest to that."

I seek out her mouth in the dark and kiss her. My palm strokes her stomach and then settles on her hip. "Your parents?"

She lets out a groan that tells me everything I need to know. "My dad's an asshole and my mother is overbearing. There. Happy?"

"No. They upset you. Why the hell would I be happy?"

The bed starts to shake and it takes me a moment to realize she's silently crying. Behind this bubbly, loud, hurricane of a woman is someone who harbors some serious pain. If anyone knows about mental anguish, it's me.

"Shhh," I murmur, hugging her to me.

She cries against my bare chest silently. This girl is too proud for her own good sometimes. I stroke her hair and offer her my silent support.

"Is there something I can do to make it better?" I ask.

Her palm pats against my pectoral muscle. "You're doing it, Will. Just keep doing it."

"No!"

I groan at the voice attached to the very naked body waking me up. "Go back to sleep," I grumble as I tug her back to me, her tits smashing against my side.

"Willy! It's seven-forty!" she exclaims, slapping my chest.

"What?"

I launch myself out of the bed and snatch up my phone from the bedside table. Sure enough, I snoozed through all the alarms.

"Fuck," I hiss.

She bursts from the bed, her round ass jiggling, and rushes into the bathroom. My cock is hard and ready for another round, but I have to be at work in twenty minutes. I pace around my room, trying to gather my bearings, when she rushes out of the bathroom. She yanks up my T-shirt from the floor and throws it on.

"I have to go," she huffs.

I stalk over to her and hug her to me. "Let me run you to work this morning. We're already going to be late."

"No can do, Willy," she groans as she pushes away. "I

can't be late. I need to go now."

"Just run home and dress really quickly," I tell her. "I work at Huffington Bank and Trust. I can be ready in ten minutes and we can ride together. You'll get to work by eight-fifteen. No big deal."

She plants a quick kiss on my mouth. "A bank. That does not surprise me in the least. But no. I need to be at work before eight. See you later." She blows me another kiss and is gone before I have time to argue.

I rush through my morning routine, only mildly irritated I missed my morning run, but thankful for my pre-set coffee maker. And within fifteen minutes, I'm showered, dressed, and walking out the door with coffee in hand to my silver Toyota Camry hybrid. I'll be late but spending the entire night with Lilith in my arms was worth it. Despite not having slept much, I feel better than I have in years.

My Bluetooth connection isn't working for some reason, so I don't get to hear my favorite playlist. I'm annoyed I have to listen to regular radio, but it's all I've got. I flip past some country because who the fuck even listens to that shit. I skim past Lilith's favorite classic rap station and land on some Alice in Chains playing. I tap on the steering wheel along with the drum beat to "Would." It helps set the tone for the day. When it then launches straight into some Soundgarden, I smile. My mind drifts to the middle of the night. Waking Lilith with my mouth between her thighs. Fuck, she's so sweet. I'm pissed at myself for not getting with her sooner. I mean, she's been my neighbor for a year. I've watched her perfect body from afar but couldn't get past her mouth and all the shenanigans she was always pulling. Now that we've fucked a few times, I'm so into her it's bordering on stalking.

Perhaps I am a stalker.

Technically, I've been stalking her for twelve god-damned months.

I smirk as I pull onto the highway.

"I was hoping if I played my co-host's favorite songs, she'd hurry her skinny butt to the station but nooooo," the deep-voiced announcer says. "She's still late—oh, look what the cat dragged in. You better have a good story, woman."

A sexy, sultry, *familiar* chuckle fills my speakers and I almost wreck my car. Lilith? What the hell?

"Big D, I was busy," she smarts off.

"Busy with what? Your hair is dripping wet and you don't have any makeup on. And wait…is that a hickey?" Big D asks, clearly amused.

She plays it off with a chuckle. "You say hickey, I say Tinderbite."

I growl as I think about those fuckers who came on my property looking for her.

"Tinderbite?" Big D questions. "Do I even want to know what that means?"

"It means…" she trails off. "Whatever. Don't judge, D. Like you haven't ever been late. *Everyone* is late. It's Monday, for crying out loud. I bet half our listeners are late and sitting in traffic on the 295."

I crawl to a halt, indeed stuck in traffic on the 295.

She continues, "In fact, let's take some calls. What excuse are you giving your boss this morning for why you were late? Does it beat 'I-was-trying-to-cover-my-Tinderbite-with-foundation-and-failed-miserably?'"

Big D chuckles. "Okay, Lil, I'll play your game. Let's see what our listeners have to say. Call us at 555-732-WXOJ and let us know."

I dial the number and wait in a queue while a guy named Brandon complains he's late because his neighbor's lawn service blocked his driveway and he couldn't get out. A lady named Gwen tells us about how her son had a blowout with his diaper and she had to bathe him before she could leave.

Boring.

Answer, dammit.

"This is Big D," he answers. "You're on the air. Tell us why you're late this morning."

"Hey, I'm Wonka. I'm late because I spent all night exorcising my crazy neighbor's demons." I yawn for effect. "It took up a lot of energy and I was exhausted this morning. Although, I could have been a little later to try one more time."

Big D snorts. "We're calling it exorcising demons these days. That's a new one. Thanks for calling in, buddy. We'll take a new caller—"

"Wait," Lilith's voice says. "I need to hear a little more of this story. She sounds like quite the temptation. Definitely worth sinning for."

Goddamn, she sounds so sultry on the air. My cock is hard.

"She does love red," I admit. "It looks pretty good on her. She just needs a saint to tame her evil ways."

She huffs. "I'm not—I'm sure she's not evil. *You* sound kind of evil. Big D, he has an evil voice, doesn't he? Probably does all kinds of crazy crap in his grandma's basement."

I cringe because she's not far off from the truth…

Big D snorts.

"Oh, I'm definitely a saint. This one is as evil as one can get. Would you believe, speaking of Tinder, she sent all her failed Tinder dates to my house. Who does that?"

Big D laughs and Lilith lets out a hiss.

"Sounds like you deserved it, to be honest," she says. "If I were her, I'd fork your yard just for being a pompous little man."

"Little?" I choke out. "There is *nothing* little about me. In fact, she likes to call me Big Willy." I pause for dramatics. "Like that big killer whale from the 90s movies. Also, she already forked my yard once." Fuck how that shit pissed me off.

Big D is laughing, but Lilith is riled up.

"Usually, if someone goes as far as to buy fifty boxes of forks, they mean business. Their victim totally deserves it. Not to mention, she sounds quite dedicated. Do you know how long it takes to put over seven thousand forks in someone's grass? All night, Wonka. All night."

I laugh. "Well, she definitely has stamina. You're right about that."

"Pig," she says. "Next caller."

"Actually," Big D tells her chuckling. "Big boss man is waving behind you to keep talking. Apparently, the listeners are blowing up WXOJ's Twitter feed. They want to know more about the naughty neighbor from hell."

"Ughhhhh," she groans.

"Do you have all day? Because I have so many stories. Would you know she 'accidentally' egged my house once?" I question.

"Accidental eggings can so happen!" she argues.

Big D roars with laughter. "And how's that? Was she on her way to an Easter egg hunt and took a little tumble onto her neighbor's porch?"

"She probably was. You're both pigs. Why are you

siding with Not-So-Big Willy over here, D? I thought we were besties," she says, irritation in her tone.

"Aww, girl, you'll always be my favorite. Tell us more, though, Mr. Wonka."

"She's super crazy and obnoxious," I explain to him. "But she kind of grows on you."

"She sounds delightful," Lilith says.

"A real peach," Big D agrees with a snort.

I hear her slap him and him say, "ow."

"I have a problem with her," I tell them, growing serious.

"What?" Lilith asks, hurt in her voice.

"I wanted to ask her out, but she blew out of my house without giving me her number. Even though she's border-line bananas, I'm quite fond of her cherry lips. What should I do?" I question.

"Awww," Big D replies. "She sounds sweet."

"Oh, she's *real* sweet," I agree.

"Anywayyyy," she draws out, embarrassment in her voice. "Maybe she'll see him later since they're neighbors and all."

"Maybe he can't wait that long. Maybe he misses her already," I mutter.

Big D chuckles. "Well, maybe he should do a grand gesture like show up at her work and take her out. I bet she's real fond of cheap beer and greasy cheese sticks. But, hey, aren't all chicks that way?"

"Well, I did learn where she works today," I admit. "It's a possibility. That would mean leaving work early, though, and I'm already late. I'm not really the kind of guy who lets his job slip to go on dates."

"Sounds like she might be worth it, though," Big D says.

"Right, Lil? She sounds worth it?"

"Totally worth it. Bye now, Wonka. Good luck with all that. And now we have a song called 'Creep' by Radiohead. Seems fitting."

The connection ends and soon Thom Yorke's voice fills the line. I'm grinning like an idiot. On the way to work, I plot out a plan to show a wild, colorful, vibrant woman like Lilith Hamilton that I know how to be fun too.

I can be so fun.

And if it doesn't work out, I'll just reintroduce her to my dick because he's definitely a fan of fun.

I did leave work early. I thought my co-workers were going to faint. It just doesn't happen. Usually, I'm one of the last ones to leave. But, today, I have something important on my agenda.

Lilith.

All day long, I thought about her. The way she mewled when I licked her just right. How she'd go quiet when I'd fuck her sweet cunt, her fingers latched into my hair for dear life. This girl is most definitely growing on me and I'm growing on her too. There's so much I don't know about her. I want to learn it all.

I sit outside her radio station, parked next to her sports car, looking very much like the stalker she pegged me as. How does a girl like her even afford a nice car like that on a radio DJ's salary? I start doing the math when she and a big fella I've seen at her house a lot walk outside a back door. She hugs him and he walks off. Her head is down as she heads toward her car, walking slightly bowlegged, I might add. But, goddammit, she looks so pretty. Even in a rush this morning, she somehow managed to pull off a look that makes me want to strip her down and fuck her across the hood of my hybrid.

She's wearing holey jeans and charcoal-gray flats. Her white tank top is sheer and reveals a hot pink bra underneath. I'm instantly jealous of every motherfucker who got to look at her all day. Her dark brown hair is now dry but messily pulled into a bun that suits her personality. She must have found some time to put on makeup because when she lifts her chin and sees me, I notice her lashes are painted black and her lips are cherry red, just how I love them.

"Wow, neighbor, fancy seeing you here," I tease.

Her smile is immediate. Shy even. Crimson blooms over her cheeks as she comes to stand right in front of me.

"You left work early," she observes. "Isn't that like Banker Boy No-No 101?"

I slide my hands to her round ass and pull her against me. "Maybe I'm a bad boy sometimes."

She giggles and angles her head up. "I'll believe that when pigs fly, Wonka. This is probably the most rebellious stunt you ever pulled in your life. I'm a bad influence on you."

I don't tell her she's wrong.

Instead, I kiss her bright red lips that are begging for attention. She lets out a pleased moan when I push my tongue into her mouth, seeking her sweet taste. We make out like a couple of teenagers in her work parking lot until her stomach growls.

"We should go," I tell her, my lips peppering kisses along her cheek to the side of her throat.

"We could stay and do more of this in the back of your Prius."

I laugh. "Don't insult me. I'm a real man. I drive a Camry."

"Excuuuuuse me," she snorts. "I stand corrected."

Tugging her keys from her hand, I pull away and stare down at her. "I'm driving your car and we're going to dinner. Hop in."

"Maybe I should go home and dress appropriately," she says.

"Nope. You're perfect. Car. Now."

She smirks at my bossiness but actually obeys. Once I'm sitting in her beast of a car, I quickly marvel over the smell of leather and shiny chrome. Sometimes being practical sucks. I'd give my left nut for a car like this.

But what about your 401k?

With gritted teeth, I peel out of the parking spot and barrel out onto the road. She laughs at my driving.

"Slow down, Vin Diesel. I'd like to actually make it to the country club steakhouse in one piece."

I raise a brow at her and shoot her a look. "You want steak?"

She blinks at me in confusion. "What? No. I thought you wanted steak and the country club seemed like a place you'd want to go with that bowtie and all." Her lips twitch at her dig.

"Nobody makes better steak than I do, so it's kind of a pointless fucking endeavor," I admit with a huff.

"Well, by all means, take me someplace that meets your impeccable standards, Willy."

I drive her downtown and we pass several five-star restaurants. She's stiff in her seat, but when I flip to her radio station and Pearl Jam belts out, she settles. I make it to a rougher side of town to a little seedy bar called Lenny's Lounge. Since it's just after five, I find a spot out front.

"I certainly didn't expect this," she says softly.

For a moment, I worry she really did want steak.

"Don't freak out, Wonka. It's a good surprise," she assures me.

I lean forward and kiss her plump lips before climbing out of her awesome fucking car. When I round the side of the vehicle, she's already getting out. I offer my hand and she takes it. We walk into the bar and the owner, Lenny, waves at us from behind the counter. I've known Lenny since I was a little teenage shit who liked to try and sneak into his establishment. Instead of kicking me out, he gave me a job balancing his checkbook in the back office. One of the few people in my life when I was younger who gave a damn about me.

"Glad you brought something to brighten up this dingy bar, Will," Lenny calls out. "What'll it be for you and the hottie?"

I guide her over to a table near the empty stage. Nobody's here yet, but Mondays are karaoke night and in another hour, this place will be hopping.

"My girl likes greasy cheese sticks and you're the king of that shit. Bring us some of those, some buffalo wings, and anything else you can scrounge up. We're hungry," I tell him.

"Only if you lose that creepy thing around your neck, Bill Nye the Bowtie Guy," he shoots back with a chuckle.

Lilith giggles as I tug off my bowtie.

"Yeah, yeah. Bring us some shitty beer while you're at it," I grumble.

We settle at a dinky high-top table and I move the ash-stained ashtray to another table. Despite being the shiniest and prettiest thing to ever set foot in this place, she seems relaxed and at peace. It calms my anxiety knowing she's pleased with my choice.

Lenny brings us a couple of draft beers in questionably clean glass mugs and then beats on the jukebox until some old Aerosmith song starts playing.

"Who knew you had the hookup," Lilith says as she sips her beer. "There's a lot I don't know about you, Wonka."

I twirl the bowtie in my hands. "I'm full of surprises."

"Full of shit is more like it," she teases, plucking the bowtie from my grip.

She wraps it around her neck and fastens it. I let out a snort because even though it looks cheesy as fuck with her hot girl outfit, she still rocks it better than I do.

We spend the next hour eating greasy food and arguing over who was the best rock band from the late nineties as the place fills up with patrons. When she utters out Limp Bizkit, I lose it and nearly spill my third beer all over my lap.

"It's six," Lenny's voice rumbles on the loud speaker, "and you know what that means."

"Karaoke!" everyone yells.

Lilith is all smiles as she turns toward the stage. The house band, The Goons, plays every song flawlessly for every request. Eventually, after a round of shots, Lilith scoots from her seat and winks at me.

"I'm going in."

I laugh and watch her ass along with every other motherfucker in here as she runs over to the stage. Another guy, a tall, lanky dude, starts for the stage at the same time. When she realizes he wants to be next, she encourages him to go up there with her and they can sing together. People cheer them on and I smile like an idiot. The atmosphere. The beer. The music. But most of all Lilith. This night is better than I could have imagined.

"Everyone, this is Jace and he tells me he is the lead singer of a band called Fryin' Pan," Lilith says into the microphone. She waves a CD. "And lucky me, he gave me his demo. Lucky for him, I'm going to play this on the radio tomorrow. You all better listen or I'm gonna come back here to give you all a piece of my mind. Ready to see if sweet Jace here can sing?"

The crowd cheers. It's amazing how she enchants everyone she comes in contact with. She and Jace put their heads together, and I see her moving her hands in animation. Then, she turns her back to the crowd and tells the band. They all nod, grinning. Soon, The Cranberries' "Zombie" starts playing, the drummer nailing the beat. People are standing, eager for the hot brunette to bring it on.

She dances in place, showing everyone how sexy she is as the song builds. Then, she brings the microphone to her lips and starts singing the lyrics. I get the fucking chills because she sounds so amazing. When the chorus rolls around, Jace brings in another layer that's deep and raspy that harmonizes with hers. The original song isn't a duet, but they make it work somehow. This crazy crowd goes nuts and some old guy with a beer belly head bangs in front.

She points at me as she sings, her sultry voice speaking to me as though we're the only ones here. I wink at her, which causes her to smile. Then she's back to singing the chorus with Jace. I can't get over the fact she's such a natural on the stage. I abandon the table and walk past a bunch of people to the stage. Soon, the song is over and she hugs

Jace. He seems starstruck and I overhear her telling him she's going to help him get his music out there. Pride surges through me.

This. Fucking. Girl.

She leaps off the stage into my arms and I kiss her sexy mouth.

"Wonka, I've had fun," she murmurs against my lips.

I drop her to her feet and grab her hand. "Fun's not over, baby."

She squeals when I lead her through the throng of people to Lenny's office. We push inside and I lock the door behind us. Our mouths fuse together as I work at her jeans. I manage to get them pushed down her thighs. Then I wrap my arm around her waist and carry her over to Lenny's desk.

"Bend over, pretty girl," I bark out.

She looks over her shoulder at me and flashes me a sweet smile before folding over the desk and offering me her ass. I pull my aching cock from my slacks and slide the tip of my dick against her wet opening. I'm buzzed, she's buzzed, and we're fucking amazing together. I push into her hard enough to make the desk scrape along the old linoleum floor.

"Oh, God!" she cries out.

I grip her fleshy ass cheeks and spread her open so I can see her asshole as I slide in and out of her cunt. When I thumb her hole, she lets out a low groan.

"One day, I'm going to put Big Willy in here," I tell her, my voice low and husky.

"You're so dirty," she moans.

"You like it," I taunt as I slam into her and slap her pale ass.

Her cunt clenches around me, so I slap her again. She fists some papers on Lenny's desk as another moan lets loose. I thrust into her hard and punishing. Each time I slap her ass, she seems to get wetter and wetter. I lick my thumb and then apply pressure to her asshole. A groan escapes her when I push it inside. I can feel the added pressure against my dick and it feels so good.

"Wonka," she breathes. "You're crazy."

I slap her ass again. "Crazy for you, demon. Now come like a good girl."

Her body tightens around me and I slowly fuck her asshole with my thumb. She pushes up on the desk and leans into me. Our skin slaps together, my balls knocking against her clit, making a beautiful noise.

"Oh, God—" Her words are stolen as her entire body convulses with her orgasm. She clenches around my thumb and her cunt milks my cock straight into my own release. I start to come, but I decide I want to paint her ass with me. Pulling out, I watch with lust-filled appreciation as my thick, ropy, white jets of cum spill all over her ass that now bears my handprint.

"What a beautiful fucking mess you are, Lilith."

Chapter Ten
Lilith

Tuesdays are for Getting High

Just when I thought there wasn't a bed more comfortable than mine, I land in my neighbor's bed two days in a row, under a comforter possibly fluffier than mine. Maybe it also had to do with the man curled up sleeping behind me, with his large hand cupping my breast while he breathes heavily in my ear.

Sex and slumber parties at Will's are the best.

I smile thinking of waking up like this all the time. It's been a while, more like never, since I've woken up to someone. But I'm totally starting to get why people have sleepovers.

I stretch my neck to get a glimpse of Will's clock. He made sure to set, check, and double-check the alarm last night, making sure we didn't have another mishap like yesterday before he shut the lights off, not needing light to ravage me. He seemed to already have my body memorized.

Just then, my stomach growls. Seeing we still have thirty minutes before the alarm goes off, I squirm out of Will's tight hold on me, having to fight twice at pulling his grip-of-steel off my boob. My stomach growls again, and I slip on a pair of Will's boxers and my bra, then tiptoe out of his room and to the kitchen.

I go straight to the fridge, wanting to wake Will up with a yummy breakfast before work. It's the least I can do to thank him for such an awesome night I had.

The problem is, when I open his fridge, I remember I don't know how to cook. "How hard can this be?" I ask myself, pushing around items in search of eggs. "Okay, no eggs." *Who doesn't have eggs?* Me, since I don't cook and entrust in those food services to deliver my premade meals.

I find a box that has a picture of an egg on it. "Egg whites," I repeat. "Hmm…eggs in a box. Okay then." I pull them out, along with some weird organic ham and some *vegan cheese*? What is this poor man eating? He eats steak, so I know he's not a vegetarian. Not sure how he ended up with vegan cheese. I'm tempted to walk home and grab us some microwavable omelets made with real ham and cheese.

I search out some pans, finding them in the cabinet below the stove. Oil, *check*. Spices, *check*. My stomach growls again, which puts another great idea in my head. "Pancakes. Pancakes sound delicious right now." I try and remember the ingredients from a Food Network show Daryl and I watched one day about breakfast, and go in search of more stuff.

I manage to cover all of Will's kitchen counters with ingredients. Placing the pan on the stove, I turn on the heat and pour a bunch of oil in it. "Okay, while that heats up, let's make the batter." I'm feeling good. Like *really* good. I haven't had a skip in my step like this for a very long time. Per the instructions, if I remember correctly, I add a cup of flour. It doesn't look like it would make enough, so I alter the recipe and add two more cups into my bowl. I remember the recipe calling for eggs, but Will doesn't have any, so I take a guess and match the flour, pouring three cups of egg white mixture into the bowl.

A loud ding sounds behind me, making me jump. I accidently knock over the milk when I turn to see the coffee maker start. "Jesus." I grab at my chest. I look around, trying to find a towel to clean up the milk, when I notice smoke coming from the pan. "Oh shit." I quickly grab the box of liquid eggs and pour them into the searing hot pan. At least they'll cook fast—

"Shit!" I yelp as the pan crackles and the egg mixture starts to sizzle and spit back at me. I grab the towel hanging over the stove handle and use it to swipe at the building smoke. The eggs crackle louder and escalate, a flame blowing up the side of the pan.

"Oh no..." That's not good. I use the towel to slap the flames, only to catch the towel on fire. "Oh no no *no*." I begin to panic. Rightfully so, since the pan is fully on fire. I turn to grab something, *anything* off the counter to stop the fire, but my hand knocks the bowl of pancake mixture off, spilling all over the floor. I squeal as the mixture soaks my feet.

"Shit!" The kitchen quickly fills with smoke.

The smoke triggers the fire alarm, which starts blaring throughout the house. I know I need to put this fire out before I burn Will's house down. *What are the chances Will doesn't wake up to this and I can get it handled first?*

I glance at the coffee pot.

Bingo.

You got this, girl.

I take the pot and throw the hot liquid over the pan.

And the fire erupts.

You don't got this, girl.

"What in the hell is going on?"

I whip around to see Will in just a pair of black boxers. Man, he looks angry. "I was just trying—"

He cuts me off by pulling me away from the stove. Once he turns the knob and shuts off the stove, he grabs the pan and throws it in the sink, hissing as he burns himself in the process.

"Uh, Will? The fire is, uh…" I can't even spit it out. Will turns to see the flames catch fire to the backsplash. He jumps into action, grabbing a fire extinguisher under the sink, and blasts the stove, then wall. We both hear the cracking of the coffee pot spilling coffee all over the base and counter.

Will points and shoots at the coffee maker.

"Open the back door. NOW," he snaps.

I jump, running to the back door and do as I'm told. A gust of smoke races out into the open air.

I turn back. "I tell ya, they really need to put better instructions on those—"

"What the hell did you do?" Will stares at the wreckage. *Uh-oh.* Someone doesn't look very happy. I also take note of the destroyed kitchen.

"It doesn't look that ba—"

"My stove is ruined. My coffee pot is ruined. Look at my goddamn wall!"

"Okay, I think you're overreacting. It's just a small—"

He throws his hand up to silence me. "Stop. Just stop." He drags his hands up his face and into his hair. He seems really fixated on the coffee pot.

"The good thing is you can replace that old thing," I say, trying to make light of the situation.

"That was a brand-new Jura 15093 automatic coffee

machine with built in expresso and milk foam capabilities," he growls.

"No big deal. I'll just buy you another one." Still trying to see the positive side of this.

Without pulling his eyes away from the destruction, he responds, "That's a three-thousand-dollar machine. I'm sure very much out of your budget."

I can't help but feel the verbal blow. My eyebrows crease in anger. I know I don't have a right to be mad, since I almost burned his kitchen down, but throwing jabs at me that he's clearly wrong about doesn't sit well with me. "Yeah, well, who says I can't? And why do you have such a silly machine anyway?"

His hands go back down his face. He takes in a deep breath. "Because that's what I prefer. Do I also need a reason not to have you set the damn thing on fire? And look at this mess. The damage. My floor…" He continues to point out the unimportant things. All things that can be replaced. Way to ask me if *I* was okay. Make sure *I* didn't get hurt, trying to cook *him* breakfast.

"Yeah, I see it. I see an accident. I see all things replaceable. But don't worry, I'm okay. No need to bother asking." I don't stick around for his response. I storm past him to the front door. I don't care that I'm just in a bra and his boxers. It seems to be becoming a thing for me to walk scantily across our front yards.

"Lilith, wait," he calls behind me, but I don't stop. Screw him. "Lilith, wait. I'm sorry—"

I slam the door on his apology.

"…And that was 'Soul Suckin' Jerk' by Beck. Definitely one of my favorites and one I can relate to today."

"Why's that, Lil?" D asks into his mic.

"Well, D, because I know a few. Which brings us to our topic today. Jerks."

Daryl laughs into his microphone, punching in a few sound effects. *"Uh-oh. What brings on the mood, girl?"*

"Oh, nothing, just thought today would be a good day to talk about it. We're talkin' about anal jerks who are r-u-d-e. The ones you mistake for nice guys. Understanding guys. But nooooo. They flip out first, ask questions later. We got any callers who know these kinds of guys? Call in."

"The lines are open. Let's hear it, Morristown. Let's call out those jerks." Daryl turns off the *Live on Air* button and plays a quick rendition of *"You Learn"* by Alanis Morissette, as the lines light up.

He begins to open his mouth and I stop him. *"Don't even."* I have *no* interest in talking about Will and that's exactly who Daryl wants to talk about.

The door to the small studio opens and Leon, our boss, sticks his head in. *"Guys, I got the ratings in from yesterday. Good work. Whatever you did, keep it up."*

Daryl's eyes light up. *"Could it have been our special first-time caller?"*

I mouth *"shut up or die."* He laughs at my expense and waves Leon away knowing, we go back live in three, two, and he clicks back on the *Live on Air* light.

"We're back, and looks like Morristown might be filled with more jerks than we thought. Our phone lines are lit up like a Christmas tree. Hello to our first caller. What's your name?"

"Christine. Love you guys. Love your show."

I lean closer to my mic. "Thanks for calling, Christine. Tell us your jerk story."

"Lil, I swear it, my boyfriend…" She pauses and we hear her sniffle. "I mean ex-boyfriend. He straight up dogged me. Told me I was no good and left me for my…my…sister." Christine breaks down crying.

Daryl plays some 'gasping' sound effects and pulls his mic close to him. "Dang, girl. Now that's a jerk! We're sorry to hear that. We're gonna treat you to a free manicure at Betty's Salon on Sixth Avenue. Tell 'em Big D and Lil sent you. Chin up, girl, thanks for calling." He lets her go and hits another lit line. "Yo, caller, what's your name?"

"Oh my God, I got through! I listen to you guys all the time!"

I speak into my mic. "We love hearin' that! Now let's hear your not so lovin' jerk story, honey."

"A coworker of mine. He's been hitting on me since I started. Finally asked me out. I said no because, you know, I don't want to mix business with pleasure, and when I turned him down, the jerk went and complained to HR that I was harassing him!"

"He did not!" I yelp in my mic. "I hope you took your shoe to his…" I lose my concentration when Kasey, our intern, starts banging on the window, holding up three fingers. I stare at her, having no idea what she's trying to tell me. Daryl turns and nods.

"Thanks for callin', honey. You need to take yourself to Manny's. Have some of his famous tacos and margaritas. Tell him we sent ya and get a fifteen-percent discount." Daryl disconnects the caller and clicks on line three. Ahhh… "Hello, caller, you're on the air. You got a jerk story for us?"

"Hey, Big D. Thanks for taking my call."

That voice.

Uptight, anal, sexy, jerk voice.

"I recognize the voice from yesterday. Mr. Wonka, right?" He smiles at me.

I scribble on a pad of paper and hold it up that says, 'hang up.' Of course, his big arrogant ass shakes his head.

"You callin' to give us an update on your date?"

"Yeah, I could use some advice from your listeners. You see, remember that neighbor I told you about?"

"Yeah, the crazy one?"

Oh no, he didn't.

I toss my stress ball at Daryl, nailing him in the forehead.

"Yeah. Well, I took your advice. Picked her up and took her on that date. We had an amazing night. I've never seen someone take down so many cheese sticks in one sitting."

Oh no, *he* didn't!

I slam my hand on the desk. "Wow, sounds like she found you boring, so she passed the time on more exciting things like gooey cheese sticks."

Will responds, "No, trust me. She had a great time. She moaned how great a time she was having in the back room of the bar. And moans don't lie."

Daryl busts out laughing.

"Lies! Next caller—"

"So, what's the problem, Mr. Wonka? Sounds like all should be good in paradise."

Will sighs loud, that overdramatic faker. "Yeah, it was until I woke up to her trying to burn my kitchen down." Oh, come on! He makes it sound way more dramatic than what really happened.

I let out an exaggerated huff. "I'm sure it didn't happen like that."

"Oh, it did."

We both hear banging on the window and see Leon motioning for us to go with it. Of course, Daryl gladly follows along. "Oh, hell no. Say again, Mr. Wonka. Your crazy neighbor did *what*?"

"I have the damage report from the fire department to prove it. I thought I gave her the night of her life. She even screamed so a few times. I was hoping maybe your listeners could help me figure out what I did wrong."

"Pfft, maybe she was trying to do something nice for you and accidents *do* happen," I bark off, tapping my fingers on the studio desk in front of me.

"I don't know. She ruined my favorite coffee maker. I'm also going to have to replace the stove. Not to mention the wall she set on fire. Should I go into what she did to my floor?"

"No!"

"Yes!"

Daryl and I answer at the same time. I'm sure it's obvious who said what.

"Man, your neighbor does sound cray cray. You sure she's worth it, man?"

I'm going to kill both of these two dimwits.

"I think so. I mean, if you saw her in red—"

I jump in before he goes any further. "I'm sure if you had let her explain what she was trying to do you may have realized she was trying to do something nice for you. But you sound like a man who flies off the handle before asking questions, Mr. *Wonka*. Am I right?"

"That you are, *Lil*."

Damn, he catches me off guard by his admittance. That's also the first time he's called me Lil. And it sounds stupid sexy off his lips. "So, am I right that maybe if you had asked what happened, you would've realized maybe she was trying to do something super nice for you since you showed her a great time last night?"

There's a stretch of silence where I fear he may have hung up.

"You still there, Mr. Wonka?" Daryl chimes in.

"Yeah. I was just thinking how she showed me more than a great time last night. I got to see a side I feel people rarely get to see from her. I saw her truly happy and at ease. I don't know how to explain it. She's becoming like a strong drug for me. I always feel high in her presence. And I know after last night I'm slowly becoming addicted to her."

Oh shit.

A swarm of butterflies flutter around in my belly.

"Wow, that's some deep stuff, homie. What would you say to your neighbor if she were listening right now?" Daryl pokes, because I'm a bit too jaw locked to speak.

"Big D, I'd tell her I was the jerk. I shouldn't have gotten so mad. You see, I'm kind of crazy myself. I like things in order you could say—"

I break in with a chuckle because liking things in order is an understatement.

"Anyway, it's like inviting a bull into a china shop—"

"Who you callin' a bull?" I cut in. Just when I thought he was saving himself. Daryl won't stop laughing and Leon won't get out of that damn window, encouraging us to keep Will talking. Little does Leon know…

"Well, listeners, sounds like our man Mr. Wonka here's in a predicament. Should he try workin' it out with his crazy neighbor?" D asks. "The one who makes him high on the sight of her? Or should he ditch her like a bad habit and

105

rehab his love life? Let's help Wonka decide. Make sure to jump onto our Facebook page and vote. We gotta cut to commercial. Thanks, Mr. Wonka, for callin' in."

I take us off air as Daryl starts playing "Your Decision" by Alice in Chains.

How fitting.

Who's Wonka?

What's his real name?

Where can they find this crazy neighbor?

The calls didn't stop. They wanted to know who the crazy neighbor was so they could avenge him or high five her. People hated her or loved her. I couldn't even imagine the fear I'd feel if anyone caught on *I* was that crazy neighbor. But then again, the mere thought of Will losing his shit over all the picketers on his precious lawn, is enticing.

So many saw him as the poor martyr. This perfect, stable guy who just wanted to show a girl a great night out. The last comment about him being high on her? Man, did our listeners eat that shit up. I did too, until those same listeners called in, one after another, stating how he should dump his *crazy* neighbor. The amount of times a caller tried blasting their phone number on air was seriously pissing me off. The problem was I couldn't tell the difference between anger and jealousy. *Was I jealous?* All these damn nobodies calling and throwing themselves at my man. *Was he my man?*

I accidently set his kitchen on fire. Keyword, accidently! I lost count of how many times I was so close to losing my cool and explaining myself on air. I also bet that my neighbor was listening all day, eating it all up. Don't get me started on how much fun Daryl was having with all this. By the end of the day I settled the debate myself. I was no longer jealous but angry and there was only one thing to be done. To get even.

Because setting someone's kitchen on fire isn't enough.

I pass on going to Manny's for half-off tacos and go home.

In the beginning of the day there was huge guilt about what I did. I know it was an accident. But his comment doesn't make it right about me not being able to afford to replace his stupid coffee maker. It's just another reason why I hate money. Why should me being able to afford it or not define how sorry I was? I did the right thing and ordered him a new one, but after the day I dealt with, I called the company back and made an adjustment.

Hope he likes his fancy *pink* coffee maker.

I pull into my driveway and notice fireman Hank's SUV parked on the sidewalk. "You've got to be kidding me," I mumble. There's no way he can possibly think my detectors are still bad. I park and get out just as Hank is walking down my porch steps.

"Hey, what happened?" Not sure how he got in my house. Crazy next door probably called in a fake fire.

"Oh, uh, hey. Sorry. I—we got a call." He tips his head to the house beside mine.

Of course they did. I eye the house next door, shooting death lasers at his clean shutters, and watch them pretend to fall to pieces. Then his roof starts caving in and—

"Everything's good, though. No fire. So…I'll just be on my way." Hank tips his cute fire hat and hurries to his car.

"Oh, okay then."

Geez, what's his problem?

He's probably afraid I'm going to jump him and force him into my house again. *That was kinda wrong,* I think to myself as I grab the mail from the small box attached to my house and walk in. I shut the door and throw my mail onto the small entrance table.

The first whiff I get, I stop in my tracks. I smell something. *Oh my God, is there really a fire?* I turn, looking out my window, but Hank's already gone. I grab the small vase off the table in case I need the water to stop a fire. I move toward the smell, and it seems to be coming from the kitchen. It smells like a lit match, or candle, or—

"What the…"

I walk into my kitchen to find Will.

He's seated at my small kitchen table. Candles are lit everywhere. Breakfast food covers every single part of my counter space. "What…is this?"

He stands, walking right up to me. He's several inches taller than me, so I have to lift my head to keep eye contact. With no fear I'll deny him, his head dips, pressing his soft lips to mine, and he kisses me. Truly kisses me.

My knees threaten to buckle, but his hand is quickly around my waist, keeping me from falling. His grip is strong. Dominating. He starts to pull away and I groan, placing my hand behind his head to keep him from going anywhere. I can do this kissing thing with him all day long.

He shows appreciation for my eagerness and lifts me, walking back over to the chair and sitting with me in his lap. When needing to breathe becomes an issue, I finally allow our mouths to part.

"How did you get in here?"

He doesn't answer me, but it all makes sense now.

"Ahhh…my gnome has a key."

Will smiles.

"And why was fireman Hank really here?"

"I ran into him at Betsy's diner. I needed a hand getting all this food here and he owed me a favor for not calling in a complaint on him."

I look at him, then it clicks. "You wouldn't."

"I would. He should've checked your detectors and left. Fraternizing while on the job is frowned upon. Our tax payer dollars pay for his salary."

"And he was here that day because *you* called."

"I was making sure you were safe. Can't have my girl unsafe over here."

I slap his shoulder. "I wasn't your girl when you called that day."

His grip on me tightens as he pulls me closer to him. "Fine. You win. I called before I made you mine, but it doesn't change the fact I still wanted to make sure you were safe over here. You're kind of a train wreck sometimes and I wanted to make sure if you ever fell asleep after one of your Tuesday drunk taco nights and accidently left a candle on or something, you'd have a fair warning and make it out."

I don't know whether to smack him for the drunk taco comment or kiss him silly for his sweet, wanting to keep me safe comment. I choose the sweet kiss, because his lips keep calling my name. When I pull away again, I ask, "What's up with all the food, though? You actually high? Is this some kind of stoner munchies binge?"

He chuckles, low and throaty. That laugh. Lord help me.

"No. It's a peace offering. I'm sorry for the way I responded this morning. It's nothing new that I have issues."

I open my mouth to agree, but he puts a finger across

my lips to keep me quiet.

"The first thing I should have done was make sure you were okay. I'm an asshole and I hope you forgive me."

I open my mouth again to tell him I forgive him, but his finger goes up, stopping me again from replying.

"I wanted to make it up to you and make *you* breakfast, but I realized I didn't even know what you liked. I didn't know if you were allergic to anything. If you preferred French toast over waffles. How you took your eggs."

"Not in a box," I grumble.

He smiles and kisses me quickly. "Noted. So, as you can see, I had no choice but to order everything. This is to show *you* just how much I appreciated our date. And what came to follow even more." He gives me another kiss, this one slower. "And while I feed you, I don't want you to stop talking until I know every single thing about you."

At that, I laugh. "Okay, now you really must be high."

"Only on you."

"*Pfft*. You don't need to sweet talk me. Food normally wins me over any time." Which is true. I kinda forgave him the second I spotted the plate of strawberry crepes.

"Good. Because Facebook said that seventy-four percent of your listeners are rooting for us. I'd hate to let them down."

Chapter Eleven

Will

Saturdays are for Savasana

I scratch my jaw as I stare at my stupid coffee maker for the tenth time since it arrived yesterday. Pink. She bought me a new machine—an exact replica of the charred piece of shit that is sitting on my garage floor now—but it's fucking pink.

The OCD part of me wanted to chastise her and return it. But since I'd already upset her once over the damn thing, I wasn't keen on doing it again. So, I called the station to regale those listeners about my crazy neighbor's newest shenanigan.

"Mr. Wonka, have you called to tell us how wonderful and beautiful your neighbor is?" Lilith goads after she lets me know we're on the air.

I snort. "Well, she is both of those things…"

"I smell a but," Big D says.

"Don't be gross, man," Lilith teases him.

"Go on," he urges. "These tales are the highlight of my day, along with every other morning commuter in Morristown."

"My girl. My sweet, sweet girl…"

"Oh, I'm liking the start of this story," she gushes.

"My sweet, sweet girl replaced my coffee maker. You remember the one she destroyed the other day?"

D snorts. "How could we forget?"

"How nice," Lilith says. *"I bet it's so pretty…being new and all."*

"Real pretty," I agree. *"Problem is, it's pink."*

Some fake audience laughter fills the line and then Big D's laughing follows it. "No, she didn't."

"Yes, she did."

"Sounds beautiful. Like her," Lilith huffs. *"You should send us a picture to put on our Facebook page. To show the WXOJ listeners just how lovely it is. I bet it'd get hundreds of likes."*

"Maybe I will," I agree. *"Should I take a picture with it?"*

"Hell yeah," D says as Lilith says, *"No."*

"Why not?" I tease.

"Because you've already got quite the fan club. I'm sure if they got a look at Wonka with his pink coffee maker, you'd have to put a wall around your house to keep all the chicks away and then you'd ruin Story Time with the Lovely Neighbor."

"Oh," I say with a grin. *"So taking a picture in my undies with my hair a mess early in the morning as I pour coffee from my beautiful pink coffee maker is a bad idea?"*

"Actually—" D starts, but Lilith cuts him off.

"Annnnnd it's time for a song. Bye, Wonka!"

The song that fills the line is "Pink" by Aerosmith.

I laugh out loud. That little brat.

"Don't even think about it," Lilith says, her hands on her hips.

"Think about what?"

"Taking a selfie with that thing."

I grab her hips and pull her to me. "Is someone jealous?"

"That the station blew up with women begging to see you in your undies? Nope, not at all. I'm just looking out for you, Willy. This is how you'll get yourself a stalker. You only have room for one of those in your life." She beams at me. "This girl."

I chuckle and kiss her bright red lips. "Whatever you say."

My phone buzzes and I see a text from Grandma.

Grandma: I'm making meatloaf. Get your big butt here or I'll be forced to drive all the way over there, grab you by your ear, and drag you all the way back. Love you!

"Damn," Lilith says, looking over my shoulder. "Your grandma is gangsta."

"You have no idea." I turn and kiss her cheek. "Want to come with?"

She blinks at me in shock. "Like meet your savage grandma for the first time? Like tonight?"

"Yeah, like that," I say with a laugh.

"I don't know, Wonka. What if she doesn't like—hey! What are you doing?"

Me: Sure. The usual time? I'm bringing a guest...hope that's okay.

"Oops." I flash her a wolfish grin.

She shoves me. "Ah! When is the usual time? I have to get ready!"

Grandma: Only if your guest is female. Also, swing by the Walmart and pick up a bridal magazine. See you in forty-five minutes!

"Wonka!" Lilith screeches. "Look at me! I can't go like this!"

I admire her messy hair that's piled into a bun on top

of her head. She's wearing old overalls probably from the nineties, a white tank top, and a pair of tennis shoes. "You look cute."

"I look like I've been renovating a kitchen! This is not meet-your-Wonka's-grandma attire!"

I clutch her cheeks and rest my forehead against hers. "You *have* been renovating a kitchen." At least she's been helping me gut the fire damage. "And my grandma already loves you."

She grins, her eyes twinkling with delight. "Wait, you've told her about me?"

"She's been rooting for a hookup for the better part of a year now," I admit.

"Fiiiiine," she draws out as she pulls away. "I'm going to run home and get ready."

"Don't get too pretty," I tease. "I can't have my grandma changing her Will tonight because she's in love with my naughty neighbor."

She taps her bottom lip. "Oooh, a Will, Will? This changes everything."

Then, she bounces out of my kitchen, taking my heart with her.

"I must say, honey, you're much prettier in person. My grandson never let on just how beautiful you are," Grandma says as she admires Lilith's red and white polka-dot dress.

Lilith preens under Grandma's praise. "Thanks, Mrs. Grant."

"Call me Babs," she says, grinning at her.

Babs?

"What in the—"

Grandma cuts me off. "Oh, William, it's short for Barbara. Close your mouth, son. I can see your tonsils."

Lilith snorts out a laugh that has Grandma grinning wickedly at me.

"At least Skippy is happy to see me," I start as I squat to pet my ex-fiancée's old dog—a dog she had to leave behind when we broke up because she was suddenly "allergic."

Skippy yaps at me and then runs around Lilith's ankles, bouncing up and down as if he wants her to pick him up. She obeys and hugs him to her chest. The little yorkie licks her face enthusiastically.

"You're so cute," she coos.

He yaps happily in her face.

Grandma makes a big show of winking at me and then mouths, "I love her."

She's just happy because this is the first girl I've brought home since Presley. I say home, but it's not really home. No, that home no longer exists.

Shame and self-loathing threaten to suffocate me. I'm tense and can't meet my grandma's eyes. Grandma must sense my mood because she pats my arm on the way to the kitchen. Lilith with Skippy in her arms and I behind her, we follow Grandma through her duplex. She claims she loves it better than my childhood home where she raised me. She says it's easier to keep up with. Over a decade later and the guilt still eats away at me.

"You okay?" Lilith asks, her brows furrowed together in concern.

I lean over and kiss her forehead, earning some neck kisses from Skippy. "Just fine. I'm glad you came."

"Sit at the table, Miss Lilith, and I'll get Will to pour us some iced tea," Grandma says as she walks over to the oven in her tiny kitchen. There's barely enough room for the three of us in this little kitchen. Her old kitchen was huge. "Chop chop!"

I find some glasses and sidestep Grandma to pour the tea.

"Your home is lovely, Babs," Lilith says as she sits down and lets Skippy back down onto the floor.

"I love this place," Grandma agrees. "Perfect for an old lady like me."

"You're not old," Lilith scoffs. "What's your secret to staying so young?"

Grandma pulls the meatloaf out and sets it on the table. "Yoga, dear. I'm a yoga master."

"Not to be confused with a Yoda master," I tease as I set the glasses down.

"Ahhh, Yoda," Grandma says with a chuckle. "William here loves Star Wars."

Lilith gapes at me. "No way."

I shrug and hold my hands up. "There's a lot you don't know about me."

She purses her lips together and a blush creeps up her throat. Last time we tried to get to know each other, we lasted about three questions before I was licking syrup out of her belly button. The breakfast. Her sexy stomach. Too many distractions. And since then, it's been a whirlwind of banging sex and trying to outdo each other on who can find the coolest dives for dinner that doesn't end in food poisoning.

"Besides," I continue as I grab the bowl of mashed potatoes from the counter, "everyone loves Star Wars."

"True," Grandma and Lilith say at once.

We all settle at the table and dish up our food. I'd worried that maybe conversation would be stiff at first like it was when Presley first came to dinner, but Lilith launches right into conversation.

"Mmmm, Babs, oh my God," she moans. "This is the best meatloaf ever!"

"Better than your momma's?" Grandma fishes. Grandma always fishes for compliments about her meatloaf.

Lilith snorts and nearly chokes on her meat. She swallows it down with her tea and nods. "I don't think my mom even knows what meatloaf is. She doesn't cook. Ever."

"Sounds like someone I know," I chime in.

She sticks her tongue out at me. "One failed breakfast, Wonka. I'll never live that down."

"You ever want to learn how to make my meatloaf, honey, I'll teach you. Lord knows Will doesn't know how." She whispers loud enough for me to hear, "All he knows how to cook is steak."

"It's the best steak you've ever had," I grumble.

"So I've been told," Lilith says with a laugh. "Is that why we eat out so much? Because we both suck in the kitchen?"

I arch a brow at her. "You're the only one who truly sucks in the kitchen…"

"Be nice," Grandma chides, thankfully missing my joke to Lilith. "She just hasn't been taught. Not everyone has a culinary goddess for a grandmother."

"Oh, here we go," I groan. "Tell her about your nine-layer chocolate cake. Do you have three hours, Lil?"

"I have allllll night," Lilith says gleefully. "I could talk about chocolate cake for nine hours straight. Are you kidding me?"

I shake my head at her. Such a suck-up, this one. I'm

amused by her efforts to please my grandma. She's adorable and I'll reward her later. With my tongue.

We carry on a conversation, the three of us, and I feel a tightness that's been present in my shoulders for years begin to unclench. This girl is doing something to me. She's getting inside me and rooting herself there. Unlike Presley who felt like an obligation, Lilith feels like a sweet treat. Something I don't deserve, but I'll gladly consume. I'm addicted to her.

After dinner, Lilith starts to clear the table, but Grandma stops her. "Oh, no, honey. Not in the Grant house. In this house, the men," she says, pointing at me. "The men clean up while the women do yoga."

Lilith starts giggling. "I'm hardly dressed for yoga."

"Yoga doesn't care what you're wearing," Grandma tells her seriously. "Yoga cares what you're wearing in here." She points to her chest. "Your center. We're going to find our center in my living room and embrace it." She waves at me. "While he does the dishes. Then, we'll all have my nine-layer chocolate cake that William loves to tease me about. He can just watch us eat it, the little snot."

"I see. I'm getting schooled, huh?" Lilith asks, amused.

Grandma nods. "I'll teach you everything my yoga instructor Lupe taught me."

Maybe later I'll show Lilith everything Lupe taught *me* when he emailed me some how-to videos. *Thanks for that, Grandma.* I still want to bleach my eyes. A grown-ass man rutting on the hardwood floors making orca sounds. I shudder. Perhaps I won't show Lilith. I'm not sure I can stomach that one again.

They disappear into the living room and I spend the next half hour cleaning up. When I finally make it into the living room, they're both sprawled out on the floor with their eyes closed.

"Ummm," I mutter, scratching my jaw. "I think you just made up this move, Grandma. Us non-yoga folks call it *napping*."

Lilith giggles but scrunches her eyes closed. Grandma, with her eyes still closed and her body completely relaxed, raises her hand and slowly flips out her middle finger.

"Savasana," Grandma says.

"And you're learning Russian too?" I ask.

More giggles from Lilith.

"It's not Russian, boy," Grandma grumbles. "It's a yoga move otherwise known as the corpse move."

"Sounds incredibly difficult," I deadpan.

Lilith snorts.

"It reduces anxiety," Grandma explains. "You should try it sometime."

"Yeah, Wonka, come play dead with me," Lilith teases as she pats the floor beside her.

Skippy runs over and rolls onto his back, his big, goofy tongue hanging out of his mouth. For fuck's sake. With a grunt, I kick off my shoes and lie down beside Lilith. Her hand finds mine and she threads her fingers between mine. Skippy abandons his corpse move position and jumps onto my chest.

"Dog," I grumble. "Stop licking me. I thought this was supposed to be calming me, Grandma."

"Skippy can sense distress. He's a human whisperer and right now he's whispering that you need to calm your big butt and close your big mouth."

"Did I mention my grandma is mean?" I ask Lilith.

"Awww," she teases back. "I think she's kinda sweet. Let

Skippy kiss away your woes."

I squeeze her hand and pull it to my lips. "I'd rather you kiss them away," I murmur.

"I heard that," Grandma says. "You're supposed to be relaxing, not planning your attempt at making me great grandchildren."

Lilith chokes and I groan.

Skippy yaps in agreement because he's just like Grandma, dammit.

We're silent for a good three minutes.

"I really want some chocolate cake," I whine.

Lilith laughs. "Me too. Did we play dead long enough, Babs?"

Grandma huffs. "I suppose we can take a break from our exercising for some chocolate cake."

I turn on my side and stare at Lilith, who's already watching me. Happiness twinkles in her brown-eyed gaze and pride fills me. Lilith is fun and zany and beautiful. I'm not sure how an anxious asshole who needs a human whispering yorkie landed a girl like her. She stands and steps over me, giving me a glimpse of her black panties.

I may not be sure how I landed her, but I'll be damned if I waste another second worrying about it.

"We better take that chocolate cake to go, Grandma. I've got some great grandbabies to go make."

Lilith bursts out laughing and Skippy yaps happily.

And Grandma?

I've never seen an old lady run so fast.

Chapter Twelve

Lilith

Saturdays are for Pussy Fights

"You are *not* going to eat all that." I watch Will pull out two large filets from their package and place them on a plate on my kitchen counter.

"I'm not. You're going to help me," he replies, picking up the bowl of homemade spices he made, and begins sprinkling them over the meat.

I shake my head. Yeah. No way. "I don't think so, that thing is huge. I can't eat all that."

Will looks at me with that devious smile. "Baby, I've seen you put bigger things in your mouth, I'm sure you'll be fine."

His head is lucky he's quick because the lemon goes zipping past him when he ducks. His laughter fills the kitchen. I pause to enjoy the magical sound, when he mauls me.

"Will! Gross! You have meat hands!" I squeal. He lifts me up, walking us to the nearest wall. His lips are pressing wet kisses to the crook of my neck. "Will…" I fade off, tilting my head to the side to allow him better access.

"Stop acting like you don't like my thick meat. I bet you're wet right now just thinking about it. The feel of it. Taste of it. The way my meat stretches you."

Jesus, I love his meat.

"Tell me how much you love my meat."

"I love your meat," I moan as his teeth scrape my skin, taking a nip at my shoulder.

"How hot are you for my meat?" He grinds his hard meat into me.

"So so *so* hot."

"Well, shit. We'd better cool you off then." He pulls off the wall, confusing me, and heads toward the sliding glass door. He walks us right out of the back door toward the pool.

"Will...Will, don't you dare...*WILL!*" I scream, but quickly hold my breath when he jumps, throwing us both into the pool. When he comes back up, breaking the surface, he's already sporting a huge smile.

"You're so gonna pay for that."

He kisses my wet lips. "Oh, good. Tell me all the naughty things you're going to do to punish me."

I splash water at him. "I'm going to hurt you."

Another kiss. "Oh yeah, keep going."

My hands go up and I tug at his hair. "Like really hurt you! You're not gonna like it."

"If your hands are on me, I guarantee, I'll *love* it." He doesn't allow me the opportunity to reply. His lips are hard on mine and he's kissing me like it's his job. And the employee of the century award goes to this guy.

It's a damn shame we've spent the past year hating on each other and not doing this instead. It's also probably why we've fucked like rabbits, making up for the three hundred and sixty-five days we missed out on. I never knew how much I'd enjoy such an uptight, anal man, who makes the bed before I'm out of it, turns lights off before we're even out of the room, insists on spreading butter on his toast only horizontally, claiming it doesn't soak into the bread the right way if not done properly.

But it's like they say. Never diss it until you try it. And I tried it. And I'm obsessed.

After our night eating meatloaf and yoga, I realized I loved his grandma. I snuck her my number before we left and told her to hook me up with some chocolate cake lessons. I felt super guilty that the slices she sent us home with ended up all over me and not as much in our bellies as it should have been. But Will got to lick me clean of the chocolate ganache icing and I shamelessly snuck a few chunks of the fluffy cake into my mouth in between moans. I never got back around to asking him about that strange mood change when we were there. There was something I felt he wasn't disclosing. It bummed me out he wouldn't tell me, but then again, I'm no better with all the secrets I'm harboring.

The ratings at the station are through the roof, thanks to Will and his ridiculous daily phone calls. Leon is ecstatic that Wonka keeps calling in. Me, not so much since now I have all of Morristown pining over my neighbor. Keyword *my*. It's a good thing that just the mention of hordes of people on his lawn for long periods of time talks him out of all his daily phone call threats. Okay, so maybe I'm the only one who sees them as threats. The entire female population sees them as temptations.

They started off super sweet. He called in on Monday to update our listeners on what an amazing weekend he had. He wooed them when he went on and on about how he took the neighbor to meet his grandma. On Tuesday, he called in, telling our listeners he wanted to surprise her with dinner and asked for suggestions on what to make her. The

Facebook poll had eighty-two percent on agreeance that a fancy pasta dish was best. He made steak. On Wednesday, he went on and on about the fancy meal he cooked and how he fed each bite to her. I rolled my eyes the entire time since we didn't even touch the filets. The minute I walked through his door, my shirt was off and we never left the bedroom. Come Thursday when he called, he needed to talk about his feelings and what this girl was doing to him. Even *I* was eating out of the palm of his hand. Just like every listener, I wanted to be that neighbor. At times, I had to secretly remind myself I *was* that neighbor. Friday's call, though, took the cake. I also told him I was blocking his number.

"Morning, Mr. Wonka, our callers were getting impatient. It's past your normal call time," D says into the mic at Will, who I know is sitting at work and not *at home.*

"Thanks, Big D, it's just that I'm stuck and need your listeners' help. I'm standing in the middle of my bedroom, staring in the mirror at this pair of boxers I'm wearing. My little neighbor and I had an argument. You see, she says my boxers are blue. I think they're green. I just don't know how to settle our debate."

He's a dead man.

The lines light up instantly. I swear people have us on speed dial as of late.

I roll my eyes, speaking into the mic, "Wonka, I'm pretty sure the neighbor is right on this one. Better just go on and hurry to work. Next call—"

"I don't know. I'm pretty sure they're green. She also said they were too tight. Do you think maybe—"

"No." Jesus, not this again.

"But if your callers could just see, maybe they would help—"

"No!"

Daryl can't keep his laughter contained. "I don't know, Lil, the lines are blowing up. Our Facebook page is filling with tons of requests, begging us to let Mr. Wonka post."

And I can't care less what those perverts want! I'm not allowing my boyfriend's junk, which is way noticeable in his too tight underwear, to blast all over Facebook. And I plead the fifth on why I just called him my boyfriend.

Will chimes in. "I agree with Big D. Let's take a vote. I really could use some hands on this. It's just too hard to do it myself."

Dead. Man.

And to make matters worse, Leon doesn't even spaz out at that inappropriate comment. He's so turned on by the spike in ratings, he probably wants to do Wonka too.

"Guys! Wait a minute! Why are we always so focused on Wonka? Why don't we ask to see the neighbor? Personally, I wouldn't mind seeing some hot legs, possibly some cleavage. Male listeners, what do you think?"

Daryl laughs. Will grumbles.

"No, I don't think she would like that."

"Oh, come on, Wonka! What? Don't want the world to see what you see? Just a peek. Let all the men, maybe women too, see a glimpse of your neighbor."

"No, sorry."

"Well, it seems Mr. Wonka isn't the sharing type," Daryl says, playing the 'wah wah' sound effect.

"Nah, I say we do it. Let's start a rally! We want to show the men of Morristown some of what Wonka gets. Come on, guys, let's take a poll, cleavage or those long legs he talks about—"

"They're green," Will says, followed by a click.

I won the battle. I felt like a winner all day long after that call. Until I got home Friday night and he attacked me. Will made it very clear he does not share. Never has. Never will. There would be no exploiting his neighbor or her perky tits, and her *fine-ass legs*, his words. He also made sure of it when he marked me with love bites and hickeys, so I wouldn't even be able to sneak a pic without anyone thinking I have leprosy.

Bastard.

We're choosing to spend the day at my house swimming and enjoying the Saturday sun. I've avoided spending time at my house all week in fear of my mother calling again. Will never mentioned the voicemail he heard, which is good. I wouldn't even know how to explain. I'd have to lie, which I really don't want to do with Will. No doubt every time I come home to get ready for work, the voicemail button is lit, my mother going on and on about coming home, my father this, my father that, and Lance, Lance, Lance. I know I should call her back. My father means every bit of his threat and I need to start taking it seriously.

I told myself I'd just enjoy the weekend with Will and then come Monday, figure out my next moves. I wouldn't bend for my father. But I knew it was that or he'd break me.

"I'm going to have to stop fucking you soon, so we can get the steaks on the grill before the sun goes down."

"Never," I pant, still trying to catch my breath and hoping he doesn't let me go. I'm pretty sure my legs won't work and I'll sink to the bottom of the pool and drown. Our day of sunbathing and swimming has turned into a sex marathon in the sun, in the pool, and on the deck. I haven't had any need for my bathing suit, since I've been naked most of the day. It's turned out to be a good thing, helping with my tan lines. Win-win.

"I can't watch another perfectly good slab of meat go to waste. I had to throw those filets out, you know."

"First off, I feel like what we just did with your meat was *not* a waste."

His hands are on my hips, tickling me.

"Ahhh! Okay! It's meat time!" I'm laughing, trying to push his hands off me.

He finally obeys and releases me.

"You may want to schedule a pool cleaning after today." He laughs and climbs out of the pool.

I take in his comment, then look around at the pool water. After what we just did in here, good call. I follow suit and climb out after him.

"You know, Wonka, these steaks better be good. All this *I'm a steak master* talk."

He turns and gives me that sexy smile. "They'll be good. And you're going to be thanking me with that sweet mouth of yours later."

"Mmmmm, double the meat, can't wait!"

He tries to swat me with a towel, but I'm quick and jump back.

"Speaking of sweet, let's get some margaritas going." I throw on my bathing suit and head into my kitchen. I dig through my pantry only to realize I must have drank all the tequila. Shocked, but then again, not, I yell for Will. "Hey, Willy, any chance you have any tequila at your place?"

"Yeah, bottom cabinet below the sink," he replies from the deck, trying to mess with the grill.

"Cool. I'll be right back!"

"Put some damn clothes on, though. I'm getting sick of Mr. Daniels getting a peep show."

I laugh at his comment. Throwing on a pair of shorts,

I head out the front door and next door. Will has gotten a little bit more lenient on leaving his door unlocked. One, because I convinced him we live in a very safe neighborhood. Also, so I could come in anytime I wanted to when I needed a booty call.

I head into his house, through the living room practically skipping. I walk into the kitchen and head for the sink, when I'm stopped in my tracks.

Björk.

My competition.

Will's damn cat is sitting on the ledge of the sink, giving me her usual stink eye. If there is one thing that's been made known it is that his cat is no fan of mine. I guess I can understand why since I took her spot on the bed, the couch, his heart. Instead of petting *her*, he's petting *me*. I'd probably hate me too.

It doesn't change the fact she has tried on numerous occasions to claw my eyes out. Jumping up from the back of the couch and clawing at my head was *not* a coincidence. Nor was the time she jumped out at me when I was taking a quick shower, making me almost slip and kill myself, or the other day when she mistook my plate of Chinese food we ordered as her litter box and pissed on my fried rice.

Will is clearly blinded by his furry fluff of love. Me, on the other hand, got it. Girls' intuition and all. His cat hates me.

"Uh, hey, kitty kitty. I just need to get into that cabinet, and I'll be on my way." I slowly bend down to open the cabinet when Björk takes a swing at me with her paw. I almost fall backward avoiding her claws.

"What the hell?"

She just sits there eyeing me.

"You have some serious issues," I snap at her and sit back up. I reach for the knob again, and she takes another swipe at me. I dodge her from scratching my face, but she manages to get a chunk of my hair and pull.

"Ouch! You stupid cat!" I swipe her right back, but she lifts her paw and stabs me with her damn claws. "Oh, hell no!" I jump for her, but she scurries down the counter. "Come here, you stupid feline. What's wrong? Mad your owner found better pussy?" Yeah, that's right. I'm shit talking a cat. "I should probably tell him I'm allergic. Wouldn't that be a shame? He'd have to get rid of you. No more kitty—"

That damn thing jumps at me. I'm literally wrestling a cat from clawing my eyes out in Will's kitchen. She gets me good across the cheek and I yelp. That's when I take her and throw her. She goes flying but lands on her feet and takes off into the living room.

"Jesus!" I hold my face. "That's right. Run away! You fight like a pussy anyway!" Forgetting the tequila, I leave, afraid of that psycho cat. I slam the door shut, debating on leaving it open so she runs away, and walk back next door, holding my poor cheek. I swear, I think I just got my ass kicked by a—

"What in heavens are you wearing?"

I whip my head down my driveway to see my parents.

Oh shit.

"Lilith, dear, for God's sake, you're practically naked."

I look down, completely forgetting I'm just in my bathing suit top and daisy dukes.

"Uh, wh-what are you guys doing here?"

"That's all you have to say to us right now? Is this how you uphold yourself? I do say, Lilith, you're getting out of control," my father scolds me. "And why are you bleeding?

You're not even safe here."

Oh, double shit. One of the many reasons I couldn't have them come here.

"Cat fight. I'm fine. And, uh—"

"Baby, hurry, I just threw the steaks on the grill. I showered too. You need bigger towels because this barely wraps around—"

Will stops talking when he notices the two people in my driveway. "Oh, sorry," Will says to them, disinterested. "We're not buying anything."

Kill me now.

"Oh my." My mother blushes.

My father's face turns beet red. "Excuse me, son? Where are your clothes?"

"Will, these are—"

"Lil, you don't have to buy anything. Are you from the church up the street? Do you have a permit to be walking through and putting fliers on doors—"

"Will!" I cry out. He finally shuts the fuck up. "These are my parents."

He stares back at them, confused. Once it officially registers what I said, shock takes over. "Oh shit, I'm sorry. I thought…"

"Can you, uh, maybe go put some clothes on?" I ask, knowing this will probably be the last time I see him alive anyway. My father is looking pretty murderous right now. It doesn't help that his wife is practically drooling. I want to turn to my mother and tell her I get it, but I don't think now's the best time for jokes.

"Lilith, you better explain," Daddy growls. "Or we are leaving here right now, and you're coming with us. Is this what you've been doing? Running around like a—"

"Okay, sorry about that." Will comes back, thankfully clothed.

I want to tell him to run while he can. But I also don't want to be left alone with them considering how mad my father looks.

Will approaches my father and sticks out his hand. "Hello, Mr. Hamilton, William Grant. It's a pleasure to meet you."

My father makes no effort to shake his hand. My mother is still ogling.

"You have a lovely daughter, sir."

Considering they just saw you practically naked, that's *not* helping.

"Daddy, this is my neighbor, Will. He's a bank auditor. A really great one too."

My father still stands there eyeing him while my mother sticks her hand out.

"Well, hello there. Tonya Hamilton."

Will goes to shake my mother's hand, but gets a surprise when she puts the top of her hand out. *Oh my God. Don't do it. Don't—*

Ugh. He does it!

My mother's eyes light up when Will places a kiss to the top of her hand.

"Okay, well, see you around, Will," I say curtly.

I take back keeping him around. He needs to go. Like now. He looks hurt that I'm trying to shoo him off. I'll explain later, hoping he understands.

"Well, what about dinner? We have plenty of steak." What I need is for him to stop digging us all in a hole. He turns back to my father. "Would you guys like to stay and eat with us?"

Okay. Actually, I'm just gonna leave. Save myself.

Do I tell Will now that I don't think Bart Hamilton has ever had a meal that's come off a backyard grill in his life?

"If you think I'm going to eat—" Daddy starts.

"The steaks! I left them on the grill, dammit!" Will turns, taking off through the house. I stare at his back, hoping for a meteor to fall from the sky and blow up Earth. It would save me from having to turn to my parents and explain.

"Dinner sounds lovely!" my mother chimes in, staring at the door Will just disappeared through. "But dear heavens, Lilith, we'll eat something a little bit more suitable."

Hmmm. What places does one pick when knowing they are taking their boyfriend/neighbor to his last meal?

Chapter Thirteen

Will

Saturdays are for Stepford Wives

"I can't believe I burned the steak," I grumble as we enter the restaurant that's way above my pay-grade. I never burned steak until I started seeing Lilith.

She's quiet and has been since they showed up. We're to have dinner with her parents and my normally chatty and flamboyant girlfriend is silent. I don't like it. I don't like them and I don't like the way she's seemed to shut down.

Not only has she shut down, but she's in full-on Stepford wife mode. Just like her mother. My sultry pinup now wears pastels and soft curls. The red lipstick has been traded for pale, glossy pink. Killer stilettoes have been replaced with nude pumps.

Who is this girl?

"Lilith," I say as we enter the fancy steakhouse.

She flashes me a fake smile, her teeth whiter and brighter than usual, and then points to where her parents are seated. Bart and Tonya Hamilton. While Lilith got ready earlier, I did a quick search on these people. Apparently, my secretive girlfriend is the daughter of the owner of Hamilton Investments, a Fortune 500 company. Multi-millionaire. An expensive brownstone in New York City and another home in The Hamptons.

And now their precious daughter is dating Will Grant. Bank auditor from the suburbs. Reformed bad boy. I have a criminal record, for fuck's sake.

"Darling," her mother says with a fake smile. They both stand to greet us.

I offer my hand to her father and this time he actually shakes it.

"Mr. Grant," he says.

"Mr. Hamilton," I reply back.

Lilith lets her mother kiss both her cheeks and I refrain from letting out an annoyed huff. I'm gentleman enough that I pull out my girlfriend's seat and let her sit before I take my own beside her.

"So lovely you two could join us," Tonya chirps, a fake smile on her lips. "Our daughter has told us so much about you."

Bart's nostrils flare. "Don't lie. She's done nothing of the sort. Last we heard, she was going to start seeing Lance." He waves his hand at me. "Not this."

I glower at him. His blatant disgust for me is getting old. "Funny," I grind out. "Lilith hasn't mentioned you either."

Bart's face turns beet red as Tonya fiddles with her napkin. Lilith shoots me a panicked look. A look. Yet, she says nothing. My girl always has something to say.

"So, a bank auditor?" Bart asks, his salt and pepper eyebrows furled together. "Is this a stepping stone toward what you really want to be when you grow up?" His words drip with condescension.

I straighten my back. "I am doing what I want to do and I'm really good at it. The very best, in fact. My attention to detail is impeccable." I cross my arms over my chest and clench my jaw. "Before coming here, I noticed that you own Hamilton Investments. Charles Britton is the CFO and has been for the past five years. How is that working out for you? Rumor has it he was asked to leave Ellis Island Equities for misappropriation of funds. They couldn't pin anything on him." I narrow my eyes at Bart. "I bet *I* could find out the truth."

Tonya gapes at me and Lilith is tense beside me.

Bart looks like he wants to murder me what with the way he grips his steak knife and the purple color of his face. We haven't even ordered yet, so I know the knife is for me and not the shitty meat he'll no doubt be eating within the hour.

"Charles is more than competent, young man. Don't you dare insinuate my company that I've built from the ground up—" he starts, but is interrupted by the waiter.

"Good evening, folks. What can I get you all?" the waiter asks.

Tonya and Bart slip back into fancy fuckers mode.

"I'll have the market fish of the day," Bart says. "Steamed asparagus as a side."

"I'll have a salad with no dressing," Tonya chirps. "Watching my figure." She bats her lashes at the young man taking our order.

Lilith makes a choking sound. "Wine. I'll have wine."

"Bring a bottle. And steak," I reply, sliding my palm to her thigh to calm her. "We'll both have filets cooked medium rare with loaded baked potatoes."

"Heavens to Betsy!" Tonya exclaims. "All that butter and cheese and sour cream! Lilith, darling, that'll go straight to your hips. And red meat is so hard to digest."

"Uhhh, just dry," Lilith corrects to the waiter.

I give the waiter a death glare and shake my head at him in warning. His eyes widen and he nods. "Right, so, um, I'll get this put right in and bring out the wine."

"The finest bottle," Bart says, puffing out his chest. "No matter the cost."

The waiter slinks off, leaving me with this idiot and his fembots. Once the man is out of earshot, Bart hisses at me. "Who do you think you are ordering for my daughter? And practically uncooked meat? We're not at Western Sizzler, son. If you're going to order red meat, then you order it well-done like a civilized human."

"Daddy," Lilith whines.

"It's okay," I assure her. I deal with assholes like him all the time at the bank. "I know what Lilith likes."

He scoffs. "Lilith doesn't even know what she likes. She is always experimenting with anything and everything." His gaze falls to her. "It's high time you stop playing around with your life and get serious."

I grit my teeth to keep from going off on him. It bothers me how she's acting around them. So unlike the bubbly vibrant woman I love.

Love?

I rub at the back of my neck and blink away those intriguing thoughts. I need to get through this dinner with her monster parents. Then, I'll reevaluate the way I feel about her. Now's not the time.

"Does Hamilton Investments have internal auditors?" I ask as the waiter returns and pours our wine.

Bart lifts his chin in a superior way. "Of course. I'm not a fool."

"Do you have external audits done as well? Perhaps on

a semi-annual basis? A company of your size and financial outreach would benefit from such audits." I gulp down my wine until I've drained my glass. Then, I straighten my bowtie and lean back in my seat with my brow arched in question.

"Not that it's any of your business," he snarls, "but no. I don't trust outsiders. Our firm practices are what have kept my investment company strides ahead of the rest all these years."

"*Legal* business practices?" I challenge.

"William Grant," Lilith bites out, squeezing my hand on her thigh before shooting me a fiery glare. At least that's a look I know and love from her.

"Of course it's legal. Don't insult me," Bart snaps.

"Who oversees the internal auditors?" I question.

"It's none of your business." He glowers at me.

"I certainly hope it's not Charles Britton." I smirk.

The table grows silent, giving me my answer.

"Darling," Tonya interrupts the awkwardness. "You should come play tennis with Daddy and me soon. Lance would love to play doubles with you. Unless William knows how to play."

I snort. "I don't play tennis. Thanks for the offer."

But at least now I know how my girlfriend has her banging body.

"Lilith," Bart grumbles. "I would like for you to stop by the office this week to go over some things. Alone."

She nods, in full-on zombie mode. "Of course."

I bite my tongue as to not make this dinner any worse. The more I challenge her father, the more she shuts down. I'm just so fucking pissed, though. I want to go off on this asshole.

Tonya carries on the conversation, babbling on about a summer soiree she's planning at their estate. I don't miss the fact she doesn't extend an invitation. Simply tells Lilith the parts she'll play. Gracious hostess. Smiling debutante. Puppet extraordinaire.

My blood boils as I seethe with anger.

After this dinner, I'm going to drill her about every single part of her past. This makes no goddamn sense. Where the hell is my little hurricane? Right now, she's barely a breeze.

The waiter brings our food. Bart saws into his prissy fish as if he's eager to actually eat the fucking thing that looks as though it might possibly still be alive. *Hypocrite.* Tonya picks at her salad and only pretends to eat. And Lilith? Lilith scrapes all the good shit off her potato and eats tiny bites.

The steak sucks too.

Fatty and dry and cooked more medium well than medium rare. My steaks are a million times better. I want to blast that to everyone sitting at the table, but I feel as though maybe I've done enough damage. I'll bite my tongue and choke down this shit.

Once everyone has quietly and politely eaten and we've passed on dessert, Tonya excuses herself to the restroom and all but drags Lilith along with her.

I'm left with her father.

All politeness flies out the window.

"Do you even see how you people treat her?" I demand, my voice low and deadly.

"I beg your pardon," he bites out. "She's behaving rather oddly because you, sir, are quite odd. Lilith deserves someone respectful and successful." He gestures at me as if I'm scum beneath his shoes. "Not this. You're wearing a bowtie, for Christ's sake, at the fanciest restaurant in town. Look around, Mr. Grant. You don't fit in here. Even with your little auditor job and mediocre suit. Face it, my daughter is too good for you."

I fist my napkin and then toss it on my plate. "Your daughter acts like a goddamn robot around you. Do you not even see that? Have you seen her actually smile lately?" I rise from my seat, glowering at him.

His face blanches and he looks around in embarrassment. "You're calling attention to us. Sit down."

Ignoring him, I pin him with a harsh glare. "She doesn't smile for you. Not truly. With me she laughs and is playful and enjoys the hell out of life. With me, she's happy."

"You're brainwashing her," he growls. "She needed a break. I gave it to her. Now, she needs stability. She needs to focus and start working on her future. Lance is a great stride in that direction. Then you show up and throw in a wrench."

"She's not going anywhere near Lance," I say, low and menacingly.

"You are not in control of my daughter," he bites back as he rises to his feet.

"She. Will. Not. See. Him." Each word is clipped. "She's my girlfriend and there's not a damn thing you can do about it."

Tonya and Lilith approach the table. I pull out a wad of bills and toss them on the table.

"We're leaving," I tell her as I grasp her hand.

Relief flashes briefly in her eyes. "Okay."

"Lilith," Bart starts, but I shut him down with a wave of my hand.

"Goodbye, Mr. and Mrs. Hamilton."

The moment the car doors close us in, Lilith loses her mind.

"What the hell is wrong with you?" she screeches, her finger pointing my way.

I blink at her in confusion. "Me? What the hell is wrong with *you*? You turned into a fucking robot at dinner."

"You don't understand!"

I grab her wrist and pull her closer to me. "Then talk to me because I don't know what to think right now. Everything about dinner was bizarre as fuck. Your dad is an asshole."

"Just take me home," she snips, yanking her arm away from me.

Thunder crackles from the distance and then the sky lights up, warning of an impending storm.

Irritated, I drive home. I don't get it. I don't understand how she just completely shut down at dinner. When I pull into her driveway, neither of us makes any move to exit the car despite the fact it's started to rain heavily.

"Lilith—"

"No," she interrupts, jerking her head in my direction. "The way you spoke to my father was disrespectful."

"Oh, come on," I bite out. "He was disrespectful and condescending to me as well."

"That's not the point! Whatever. I'm done talking about this."

At this, I laugh, the sound dark and annoyed. "Of course you are. You never want to talk about anything. Nothing serious. You change the fucking subject. You know why, babe? Because you hate them."

She reaches up to slap me, but I grip her arm and haul her to me until our faces are just inches apart. "I don't hate them," she defends, her glossy pink bottom lip wobbling.

"I do," I retort. "And I wouldn't judge if you did. They're awful to you."

"You were awful to me at one time," she hisses out.

"Why didn't you tell me about them? You let me walk right into the hornet's nest."

Her nostrils flare. "For the exact reason of what happened tonight! Why couldn't you just play it cool and go along with it. Daddy just likes to hear himself talk. Then, we move on. Simple. Been doing it for years."

"Are you fucking kidding me right now? Listen to yourself, Lilith. I don't know what kind of man you had me pegged for, but I'm certainly not the type of guy to sit around and be talked down to. Furthermore, I refuse to let my girlfriend's parents railroad her." I run my thumb along her wrist. "Why do you let them do that to you?"

Tears well in her wide brown eyes and she quickly blinks them away. "Because that's the way they are. And now… now you've ruined everything."

"He has no control over you," I snap.

"That's where you're wrong."

I study her face as her fiery personality struggles to break through the plastic bullshit shell she's been in all evening.

"I just hate the way you acted around them," I admit softly. "Not the Lilith I know."

She tugs her arm free. "You don't know the entire Lilith then."

"So fucking let me," I snap. "Let me in and show me how you can be that person and this one in the same body.

Talk to me."

I watch her defensive walls go up.

"Because you're so forthcoming with your past? I'll get right on that," she says snidely. "Why is it that you get touchy about your grandma's house?"

Ice forms over my heart. "We're talking about you right now. We can discuss this later."

A hollow laugh bubbles up her throat. "Exactly. What are we even doing, Will?"

"What do you mean?" I demand. We're doing everything. I can't hardly fucking live without hearing her laugh or seeing her each day. We're doing everything, goddammit. She knows this.

"Well, since you don't have an answer," she bites out. "We're fucking. That's it. You're a great lay, but we're both obviously guarded people. I can't—I can't do this with you. See you around." With that, she slings the door open and steps out into the pouring rain.

Fuck that.

I climb out of the car and charge after her. My arm hooks around her waist before she can reach her porch steps. The rain soaks through her prissy dress and clings to her gorgeous curves.

"Lilith," I plead as I pull her against my chest. "Please…"

Her tone is cold as she peels herself from my grip. "Good night, Will."

With the punishing rain pounding down on me, I watch my woman walk into her house. Alone. Without me.

"We're everything, baby," I call out.

The rain drowns my voice and takes my heart with it.

Chapter Fourteen
Lilith

Sundays are for Hangovers

I throw myself against the closed door, soaked to the bone and shivering, just as I hear his final words stab me right in the heart. *We're everything, baby.* If he knew *everything* about me, I'm sure we wouldn't be *anything*. The person he saw tonight and hated was only a smidge of the person I'm forced to be around my parents, when I'm in the clutches of the Hamilton legacy.

When I left home, my mission was to find the person I was meant to be. There was always that ache inside me that told me I wasn't on the right path. The piano lessons, the tennis, the tea parties, and fancy clothes, it just wasn't who I was inside. I was living this life on autopilot. My happiness was suffering and as much as I tried to explain it to my parents, they didn't listen. It was always the same response. The one from my father always ringing like a bell tower in my head.

"You're being childish, Lilith. You're in line to have a wonderful life. You'll want for nothing. Show some appreciation that you were born into this privilege, instead of one of many who have less."

"Daddy, it's not about the money or wealth. It never has been. I don't need special tutors or fancy things. I need to be happy."

"Nonsense. You're just fine. Everything that's planned for you will make you just as happy."

"Forcing me to be a person I don't want to be? Marrying someone I don't nor will ever love? That's not happiness, Daddy. That's an unwanted life. I won't do it. I can't."

"Maybe I should tell your tutor to teach you a lesson on how to be more grateful for what you have. You will see it one day. And you will understand we know what's best for you."

"I won't do it, Daddy. I won't."

"You will because if not, you will be far unhappier with the consequences."

I'm not sure how my father finally agreed to me having one year of freedom. I know my mother had a huge hand in it. But there's no mistaking the stipulations that were set in place. I'm sure there were ones my mother failed to mention. Deals she made with the devil in hopes that after one year I would come to my senses. See how the real world functioned and come crawling back begging for the life they wanted for me. I'm also sure my mother didn't expect me to last the full year.

When I moved to Morristown, it was like a breath of fresh air. People didn't know who I was or try to be nice to me because of my last name. Some were rude to me. And I loved it! There was no ass kissing or fakeness to people. I got rid of my fancy dresses and scarves and traded them in for red heels and bright outfits. I laughed the whole way home after buying a ton of pinup dresses, holey jeans, and tank tops from the thrift store in town. If my parents could have seen, I'm sure their eyes would have bled in disgust.

I didn't plan on getting a job at first. But when I saw the radio jockey ad posted on a job board while walking through the town square, I ripped the small piece of paper holding the contact number to the station off. I didn't have any background in radio, but I had a personality that would bypass any list of experiences. I was hired on the spot and the rest was history.

In the months to come, I transformed into someone I felt was always hiding on the inside. I became *me*. I was finally living a life that made me happy. I was finally free. Well, as free as I could be without thinking about what was to come once my year was up.

And it is.

The problem is, I can't see myself going back.

But I don't know if that decision is something I can make. At least not without tons of consequence as my father has made clear on many occasions.

I pull myself off the door and head straight to my liquor stash. I don't bother with a glass, just pop off the cap and throw a heavy gulp back. Recapping how horrible the dinner just went, I continue to swig to help my mind settle. But it never does. How could he just go off on my father like that? All those challenging questions about his work and staff? He had no idea how much worse he was making it for me. If there was any chance my father would accept Will for the person he is, it was dead and buried now. I knew that look. The look my father held when he wanted to destroy someone. And I knew he had the power to do so.

My immediate anger at Will for sabotaging any ground we had to stand on is clouding any other reason I can think of for why he did what he did. After the shit he pulled, there's no way my father is going to allow me to stay. He'll do just as he threatened and drag me home. The life I'm living will soon be a faint memory and I'll end up doing exactly as I'm told. Just when I'm falling for something real, he had to go and ruin it for both of us.

Warning labels.

They should be on everything.

Most importantly, liquor bottles.

WARNING: Alcohol is not meant to overindulge when you get into a fight with your neighbor boyfriend, which you said wasn't your neighbor boyfriend, and say things you don't mean, and do things you may regret in the morning.

My alcohol-infused anger kicks up a notch. I pick up my phone to start sending off a text rampage, when I realize I don't even have Will's number. I guess being neighbors, it was something we never needed before. But thank goodness for the Internet. I pull up Google and search for the one and only. The only problem is there are three William Grants listed. The only option is process of elimination. Starting with the first listed cell number, I fire off a text.

Me: Why did you have to open your fat mouth? You've ruined everything!

555-435-9586: Who is this?

I'm going to assume Will would know it's me. Wrong number. I take a swig and move down the list.

Me: You have a fat mouth! You ruined everything! Thanks a lot!

555-987-0967: Bitch who is this? Is this the girl my man's been texting? I'll fuck you up bitch.

Okay then. Strike two. Another swig and another text.

Me: I hate your fat mouth! Thanks for nothing!

This one doesn't reply as fast. So, I fill the time by enjoying my whiskey. The problem is, the more I drink, the more the whiskey is telling me to keep typing.

Me: What? You have nothing to say? No apology for sucking?!

Me: Don't act too good for me now! You weren't too good for me when you were fucking me all over your neat freak house!

Me: Why did you say I was everything? You don't even know me.

Me: Maybe you do. You may be the only one who truly does. It's the person I'm hiding from you that you won't like.

Me: You know what? Fuck you. Have fun sucking your own dick, asshole!

555-334-0923: Don't know what your man did to you, baby, but I'm more than willing to let you suck my dick for some attention.

So, William Grant, my neighbor, is unlisted.

Tears of aggravation pour down my cheeks as I try to rein in my emotions. I feel so hurt by everything and everyone. My parents for not wanting happiness for their only child. With Will for not understanding. I'm disappointed in myself for not standing up to my parents like I should've. The anger, sadness, confusion has me drinking more whiskey than I should. It's also clouding my thoughts. I'm struggling to separate my anger toward my parents and toward Will. I'm just so damn angry and I feel cheated. And the way this whiskey is going down, I have a feeling I'm going to be the maddest at myself in the morning.

Warning Label: Buddying up with booze will not make your situation better.

I'm lying in my bed feeling like death and mad at myself for not closing the blinds before I passed out last night.

A foul stench has me rolling to the other side of my bed. Another missing warning: *Drinking while mad is not the answer because if you drink too much you may end up barfing in your nightstand drawer.*

I throw my comforter over my head, refusing to accept the hangover that's kicking in. I'm also hoping the tidbits of last night were just a bad dream. Or I should say the stuff I remember. I wish I could say that after the failed text messaging I took myself to bed. But that's far from where my night took me. I'm not proud of what I did. At least of the stuff I remember. Trying to get Will's attention, I ran outside in the pouring rain with the intentions of letting all the air out of his tires. I laughed the entire night at my brilliant idea. What I didn't factor in was how heavy the rain was coming down and my inebriation. I ended up slipping in his lawn mid dash and landing in a pile of muddying water. This had me aborting my bright idea and taking my bruised butt back inside.

Being unsuccessful with my plan to get Will's attention, I focused my anger toward my parents and proceeded to order a dozen Pizza Hut pizzas to their residence. The look on their faces at the fear of what the neighbors would think when they saw a low-grade food chain service delivering to *the* Bart and Tonya Hamilton had to have made me feel better.

But it didn't.

I thought about kidnapping Will's evil cat. The thought made me feel better, but then I remembered I hated that furry devil thing and changed tactics.

The later the night got, the more I craved for Will. I wasn't mad at him. I was mad at myself. He was just defending me. Something no one has ever done before. I knew we were more than just fucking. We were two hurricanes colliding into a beautiful storm. He was starting to mean so much to me, and I just wanted the chance to explain myself and tell him just that.

I thought about calling the fire department to get his attention. Clearly, my drunk self was getting desperate. But the 1 percent of sober thinking that still worked told me that was a bad idea. I just wanted Will to barge through my door and force me to talk to him. Tell me he wouldn't care I was secretly a debutante drop-out. Understand I wasn't in control of my own life and he'd still love me and have amazing sex with me even after I was forced to marry a comb-over loser. A strange drunk thought had me considering it. Win-win for me and my parents. Booze will have you considering crazy things.

But he never did.

And I was running out of legal ideas to get his attention as well as the ability to see and walk straight. I was at a loss. So, I let whiskey take the wheel.

Once the rain finally let up, I went back outside and took a sharp pair of scissors and cut a heart into his lawn, but nothing.

I walked back and forth outside singing, "I'm singing in the rain" in my bra and underwear, waiting for him to spot me and furiously carry me back inside, doing me all night long until we both screamed orgasms and forgiveness, but still, nothing.

The last thing I remember was turning on the hose to water the heart because I knew he was going to shit bricks when he saw the damage to his precious lawn and I didn't entrust the downpour of rain to do the job, so my drunk self thought watering it would make it grow faster. The problem is I don't remember ever turning off the hose.

I feel buzzing under me and realize I'm lying on my phone. I reach under and grab it. Please be Will. I know it won't be since he probably doesn't have my number either. With one eye open, I look at my screen to see a few missed texts from D, my mom, and some randoms. It seems after my blackout, I spent a solid amount of time texting. Shit.

Me: D! Sup motherfucker! You awake? Bring me tacos.

Big D: I'm with my girl, Majick. Have your man get you tacos.

Me: NO! He's not my man. I think he hates me. He doesn't understand me. But you do. Tacos understand me.

Mommy Dearest: Dear Lord, Lilith. What did you send to our house? Your father is very upset with you.

Me: No idea what you're talking about.

Big D: Trouble in paradise? Save it for the show. I could use another raise.

Mommy Dearest: Don't play coy with me, Lilith, you used our credit card. We know it's from you. What will the neighbors think?

Me: That you love cheap sausage. Lolololol get it? Sausage? lololol

Me: No! Come and get me. Let's go get tattoos. Matching tacos.

555-334-0923: Does your silence mean you're not sucking my dick?

Thankfully I seemed to have passed out before replying to the last one. The text that just came through is from D.

Big D: How you feeling? Figured you were drinkin' since you tried to Facetime me over a dozen times. What's up?

Drinking seems to be an understatement of what I did last night. I can feel it in my head, my eyes, and the horrid stench in my room that today is going to be dedicated to my killer hangover. I have a weak stomach, so I'm not sure who's gonna clean up the barf in my drawer. I send a quick text back to Daryl.

Me: I need a referral to someone who cleans up disasters.
Big D: Dang girl whatchu do? Like a crime scene cleanup?
Me: I can't say. If I did, you'd be my accomplice.

I get up and shower. I may have puke in my hair that needs washing out. After spending almost thirty minutes trying to sober up and feeling no better, I get out, throw on a robe, and head toward the kitchen in need of some aspirin.

"Holy fuck," I gasp, looking at the disaster of my kitchen. Pretty sure every single condiment I own is sitting on my island counter. Food is everywhere. Pots, pans… "What in the hell?" Apparently, my inner Julia Child tried coming out last night. I walk in farther, investigating the mess. And apparently Julia wanted to make her own tacos.

The smell hits me and my stomach clenches. I throw my hand over my mouth and turn around, heading far away from the wreckage once resembling my kitchen.

I know the pit in my stomach isn't just from the bottle of whiskey still swishing in my belly. It's because of how I treated Will. None of my tactics worked last night, so it looks like I'm going to have to do it the old-fashioned way, by knocking on his door and saying those two grown-up words, I'm sorry. Because I am. I was a jerk. It's not his fault I'm living behind all these lies.

The thought that Will won't accept my apology sits heavy on my heart as I change in a pair of red shorts and a bright white tank top. I make sure to wear one of my best push-up bras in hopes it helps with his decision when I go groveling for forgiveness. I shoot a text over to Daryl, telling him I'm serious about that disaster cleanup contact, because I have to add my kitchen onto the list, covering my mouth so I make it outside my house without barfing from the stench.

The bright sun stabs me in the eyes the moment I stop outside. A part of me tells me to go back inside and sleep off this hangover. My pores are probably still seeping booze and my appearance alone is gonna have Will throwing me off his porch. Speaking of, my eyes catch movement from next door. I turn to see a small, dainty woman, beautiful no less, walking up Will's porch stairs and knock on his door.

"Who the hell is that?" I mumble, hoping Will doesn't answer. The last thing I need is for him to look at how perfect and put together that bombshell is, then follow up with the hot mess I am right now.

Don't answer. Don't answer. Don't answer.

That hope dies when I hear his door open and Will steps outside. I press my back against my front door in hopes they can't see me. My ears are perked trying to hear what they're saying, but they're not talking loud enough. *Dammit!* Who is that? My mind is suddenly all over the place. My thoughts are from a Tinder swipe to praying it's his cousin. He wouldn't already be moving on, would he? It was just a fight. Right?

The woman takes a step closer. *No, no, no...* She goes in, lifting her arms, and they hug. Okay, so cousins can still hug like that. I lower myself to my knees and crawl across my porch to the stairs. If I can just get a little closer maybe I can hear what they're talking about.

Like a snake, I slither down the three porch steps and press myself against the bushes in front of my house. Mr. Daniels is sitting in his rocking chair across the street staring at me and I put my finger over my lips for him to be quiet.

From all the peep shows he's received lately, he owes me.

I make it to the corner of my bushes when their bodies are back in sight. They're no longer hugging, which I'm relieved about. He has yet to invite her in, which also makes me feel better, but they're still standing too close for my liking.

I stretch my neck out in hopes to attempt lip reading, but the sun is making it hard to focus, on top of my clouded brain.

If I can just get a little bit closer.

Maybe just a few more feet.

I hold my breath and as sneakily as I can, I crawl past my driveway and make it into the grass. My hands and knees immediately sink into the flooded grass. *Geez, how much rain did we get last night?* "Shit." So, there's a reason I don't remember turning off the hose. Because I never did. Will's lawn is flooded. I turn to go turn the water off when I hear her.

"How've you been?"

My ears perk once again, completely forgetting about turning off the water. I don't hear Will's response, which bums me out. I could really use that information right now.

"I wanted to talk," the woman says.

His voice is low as he replies, but I can't make it out.

I need to get closer. Hear him call her his cousin and then I can go back home and maybe wait for the sun to dry out his lawn a little bit before making another attempt to apologize. I start to move, crawling through the lawn and crossing over to Will's yard. The ground is sloshy underneath me, making it hard on my incognito skills. Once I'm hidden in front of Will's front bushes, I finally hear him.

"You didn't need to come all the way over just to tell

153

me that." Dammit! Tell what? "I'm not in the mood to deal with this today." Okay, they need to start being more specific here.

"I know, but you didn't return my call."

I'm going to say that's a good thing? But then again, that would be a rude thing for a cousin not to do.

I need to get closer. I need to see how he's looking at her. I crawl along his bushes when I hear the faint sound of evil.

"Oh, come here, Björk sweetie," the woman says, followed by meowing. She knows his cat. Not a good thing. And it doesn't sound like that cat is trying to claw her eyes out. Also, not a good thing. "Have you been a good little kitty?" she purrs to the damn feline.

"Good my ass, psycho puss," I whisper under my breath.

That damn thing must have heard me, because I hear the woman struggle to keep hold of the cat and before I know it, psycho puss is down the steps and staring at me.

"Get out of here," I whisper, swiping my hand at her, but she doesn't move. Matter of fact, she hisses at me.

"You need to leave," Will says, his voice sounding stern.

"Can we maybe do lunch sometime? Maybe we can visit your grandma. I miss Skippy too."

I must admit, I'm not feeling too good about this chick. She seems to be in with all the right folks. Even the damn cat likes her. Björk hisses again.

"Now's not a good time, okay?" Will grumbles before whistling. "Björk, come here, girl."

Thank God. I give Björk a wave, telling her to beat it, but she doesn't move. She takes a menacing step toward me.

"Beat it. Listen to your daddy," I whisper, trying to shoo her off. With no luck, she takes another step closer.

"Björk, where are you going? Get up here," Will says, his voice sounding closer. Shit. If he grabs that damn cat, he's gonna see me. I'm not sure how I'd really explain this one.

"Get, go to your owner," I hiss back at her, trying to pluck grass from the lawn and throwing it at her. Maybe this was a bad idea. Yes. Bad idea. Knowing it's time to abort, I give Björk the middle finger and turn to crawl back home.

That's when that four-legged fucker attacks me. They say never turn your back to your enemies, which is exactly what I do. Just as I turn to book it back to my house, Björk pounces. She gets a good grip on me, her nails digging into my back. I forget my spy mission and make myself noticed when I scream.

"Lilith?" I hear Will's voice as I throw his cat off me. She takes off back up the steps. Trying to quickly stand, I slip and slide and fall onto my butt. "What are you doing down there?"

I look up at him, then at his better-be cousin. Dammit, she's pretty. "I, uh, I was just looking for something…I lost. I lost something."

He looks tense. Not very happy to find me on his lawn fighting his cat. It's then he notices the swamp in his lawn. "What the hell?"

"Oh yeah…What a storm last night, geesh." I make another attempt to stand, but my footing slips again and down I go.

"Jesus, let me help you," Will says, reaching for me.

I look at his visitor and see no family resemblance. Not good.

I swipe away his offered hand. "No, I'm good. You can just go back to whatever it was you two kids were doing."

Another attempt, and negative. I slip again, almost throwing me into the splits.

"Um, maybe I should go," the woman says.

"Great idea," Will replies with a scowl marring his face.

She raises her hand to touch his shoulder but thinks twice and lowers it. "I'll call you later, okay?" she says to Will, but he doesn't reply.

He's too busy staring intently at me. With how mad I'd have to guess he is right now, I'm actually considering leaving with her. The woman doesn't say anything else. It seems she knows when to also keep quiet. Without another word, she turns and walks to her car. Once she pulls away, I know it's my cue to hit the road.

"Yeah, great idea. I'm just gonna head back home. I have Sunday chores and—"

"Give me your damn hand."

I'm not gonna lie when I say he's a little intimidating right now. He looks pretty intense and I'm not even sure he's noticed the fancy heart design in his yard yet. I debate on flipping onto my stomach and swimming back to my house, but that look.

"Yep, hand, here you go." I throw my hand out and he grabs it tightly, pulling me up, and like a sack of potatoes, he tosses me over his shoulder.

"Whoa!" I squeal, not expecting his sudden move. "Seriously, it wasn't me. I saw a gang of kids with scissors and hate in their eyes. You really should call the HOA— *Ouch!*" I yelp as his open palm smacks against my butt cheek.

"Just stop talking." He carries us inside his house. Which fares better for me, since I know he's too anal to get blood all over his own house. Killing me is definitely out of the question. Once we're inside, he flips me back and holds me as I land wobbly on my feet.

"Will, I—"

"Take your top off."

"What?" Okay, maybe he's more anal than I thought. No stains.

"I want you to take your top off. Then I want you to step out of those shorts. I want you naked and ready, and when I'm done telling you how sorry I am for last night, there will be nothing between us when I fuck you right here. Right up against the front door actually."

Holy smokes.

"Well?" he asks.

"Well, what?"

"Let's get started. I can't hold off much longer not touching you. Did you want me to go first?"

I seem to have lost my voice. So I nod.

"Fine." He walks up to me, helping me raise my arms, and pulls my wet tank top up over my head. "I'm sorry for being a jerk last night to your parents." My top gets tossed and he's kneeling, his hands latching around my shorts. "I'm sorry for making accusations. And I'm sorry I didn't allow you the chance to explain." My shorts are shoved down my legs along with my underwear. "Most important-ly, I should've stopped you from running away last night. I should have never allowed you out of my sight." His palms cup my ass and he pulls my hips forward. His mouth is on me, rough and hard. My hands fly out, grabbing at his head for support.

"Oh, God," I moan, threading my fingers into his hair.

"Tell me you accept my apology." He opens me wide as he urges my thigh over his shoulder, and his tongue thrusts inside me. "We're going to talk this out, but right now, tell me you forgive me for the way I handled last night." In and out he uses his tongue to fuck me. His grip is tight on my hips. "Tell me, Lilith." He growls, adding a finger.

I moan, pressing his face closer to me. "If this is how you apologize, I'm gonna have to get mad more often."

It's then he goes to town eating me as if I were his only meal. From his finger to his tongue, he thrusts in and out, licking, suckling until my legs begin to shake. Just as I'm about to explode on his mouth, he pulls away.

"Wha—what are you doing? Don't stop." I'm panting, seconds away from having an explosive orgasm.

"I'll be glad to help you," he says, smirking. "Just as soon as you explain what the hell you did to my lawn."

Chapter Fifteen

Will

Sundays are for Starting Over

Things are weird.

Really fucking weird.

But I can fix them. I will fix them. With her sweet cunt still fresh on my tongue and her pretty pouty lips pressed against mine, I find new resolve.

We fucked up.

But we're here now. Trying to fix things.

I grab her ass and lift her. She wraps her slender legs around my waist without breaking our kiss. My sweet Lilith feels perfect in my arms. Last night was fucking torture lying in bed knowing she was so upset with me.

I should have gone to her.

But I couldn't. Lilith is stubborn as fuck and I knew she needed to cool off before we could move forward.

"Lil," I murmur against her mouth as I fumble up the stairs to my bedroom. I'd told her I was going to fuck her against the door, but I don't want to rush this. I want more than just sex. I want to talk to her because I wasn't lying when I said we were everything.

"Hmm?"

I step inside my room and she slides down to her feet.

Her brown eyes search mine. Red-rimmed from crying last night but hopeful. I want to make it all better. "I'm so fucking sorry."

She smiles. "Me too." Her fingers go to my T-shirt and she tugs it off me. Then, we work together until I'm naked too.

"Your bed is still unmade," she marvels as she crawls into it, her ass bared to me. "I thought Sundays were for chores?"

I grip her hips and flip her onto her back before lowering my body over hers. My cock is hard, sandwiched between us, but I just want to look at her for a minute. Her playful expression falls when I tenderly stroke her hair from her face. "Sundays are for starting over."

"Will," she murmurs, her nose turning pink and her eyes growing watery.

"Shhh," I whisper. "We're fixing us."

She nods and a tear streaks down her temple. I swipe it away with my thumb and kiss her softly. We kiss slowly, taking our time, as we appreciate what we'd missed. One night without her and I feel as though it's been weeks.

"I missed you so fucking much," I groan against her lips.

"I missed you too."

Her fingers scratch my shoulders and she spreads her legs. I slide my cock between the lips of her pussy, teasing her still sensitive clit. She gasps, but then a moan escapes her when I push into her. Not hasty or rushed. Slowly. Achingly so. I want to feel every part of her wrapped around me. Her body misses me because it's as though I'm being sucked inside of her tight, wet heat.

"Jesus," I groan. "You're perfect."

Her fingers slide into my hair and she blinks at me. I'm

fully seated inside of her, but I don't move. I just watch her watching me. So many words passed between us with one look. Cradling her cheek with one hand, I admire how beautiful she is. Not just on the outside but her. Everything about her speaks to all the parts of me. She's funny and sweet and crazy.

I love her.

I'm stunned by this revelation and I'm not man enough to admit it. Not after our fresh makeup. When the time is right, I'll tell her and hope to fuck it doesn't scare her away.

"So serious, my Wonka."

"So beautiful, my demon."

She giggles and her cunt clenches around my cock. It spurs me into action. I start bucking into her. Hard and uneven. My mouth hovers over hers, open and breathing her in, but we don't kiss. We're inhaling each other. Lips brushing against the other and just relishing in the softest of touches. It makes me realize how I've taken her for granted. She makes me crazy fucking obsessed with her.

"Will...I..."

"I know," I breathe against her.

I love you too.

Slipping my hand between us, I find her clit and rub against her, eager to draw out another orgasm from her. As soon as I touch her, she moans and her pussy clenches in response. Our mouths finally decide to mate and I kiss her as though our lives depend on it. My thrusting becomes harder and more intense. The headboard slams loudly against the wall. And for once I'm not worried if it'll leave marks that I'll have to patch up. Lil and I could bang right through it and I'd just be happy she was in my bed again.

"Oh, God," she cries out, her body flying off the cliff of

bliss once more.

Seeing her lashes flutter and her back arch off the bed has me groaning out my release. My cock pumps into her, my cum hot and furious as I fill my sweet Lil up. Knowing she's full of my seed has another groan of pleasure escaping me. When I'm completely spent, I slide out of her and fall onto the bed beside her. She squeals when I pull her against me. Her full tits smash against my ribs. I love having her right here in my grip, my cum leaking out of her and making a mess of my newly washed sheets.

Her fingertips dance along the grooves of my pectoral muscles and she sighs happily. I love how she relaxes against me, fitting into the space of not only my body but my heart.

I'm never letting her go.

"Who was the girl?"

All happy thoughts drain from me, and my gut feels as though it's hollowed out.

"Nobody," I grunt.

And that's the fucking truth. Presley is nobody to me. Not anymore. She told me things this morning—probably things she thought I wanted to hear and maybe at one time I did—but I wasn't interested. Not when I have this.

"Will," she starts, but I grab her hand and kiss her palm, distracting her.

"Nobody," I breathe against her flesh. "Compared to you, nobody." I pull her on top of me so I can look in her eyes. "I'm so damn intoxicated by you, Lilith. All the shit I used to care about or worry over doesn't matter anymore. Last night, you were the only thing on my mind. I sat up here all night wondering how I was going to win you back. Your parents pissed me off so bad. They don't see you like I do. Like a bright, shiny star glittering in my sky. The only star I see. Sure, there are billions in the sky, but you're the only one fucking shining brighter than the rest. You're brilliant and talented and funny as hell. For people who are supposed to love you to not see that, it was maddening. I still can't wrap my head around it, babe. Why don't they see you like I do?"

She blinks away tears and bites on her plump bottom lip. "I don't know." Her voice is hoarse and unsure.

"Well, I fucking see you," I growl, my palms running through her silky hair. "I see all of you and it's all I see."

"For a nerdy bank bouncer, you're really quite poetic," she says playfully, tears still glistening in her brown eyes.

I lift up and press a kiss to her lips before relaxing again. "You asked what we are last night." My brows furl together as I run my thumb along her jaw. "We're everything, Lil. Fucking everything."

"Okay," she murmurs. "Why don't you tell me anything about your past? How can we be everything if you don't tell me anything?"

I frown at her. Admitting who I used to be to this woman is difficult. "I wasn't a good person," I say, my voice husky with regret.

Her fingers brush against my lips. "I don't believe that."

"I was a fucked up teen," I admit. "Gave my grandma all kinds of shit, Lil. Got in so much trouble. Until I was in my early twenties, I was pretty much wasted all the time. A loser, baby. I was a loser."

"You could never be a loser," she murmurs. "I mean, look at you. You're like Mr. Perfect."

My past sneaks up behind me and tries to strangle me. I find it hard to breathe. The memories are as vivid as the day it happened. I'm suffocating.

"Hey," she coos. "Hey, look at me. You're panicking there, Wonka. Don't panic."

I lift my gaze to her soft one, my heart rate slowing. "I just can't be that person anymore. I work every goddamned day so I will be better. I owe it to everyone, especially my grandma."

She kisses me. "Well you, my friend, are doing one helluva job, I must say. I think you're pretty amazing."

"You're my *girl*friend," I correct her. "Not friend. Girlfriend. My goddamned woman. The end."

"Who knew you were such a caveman, Willy?" she teases, but her eyes tell me she's pleased.

"You like it," I challenge. "We're together and your dad can just sit on that and spin."

She snorts and slaps my chest. "I can't believe you just said that!"

Smirking, I shrug. "I'm just saying he can get over it. You're mine. He can want his little princess to marry some prince with a country club membership, but she's attached to a banker with a big dick."

"Will!" she cries out. "You're such a nerd."

"I also bet the little prince didn't win yard of the month four years in a row," I muse aloud. "Horrible yard and a tiny dick. What an awful hand he's been dealt."

She lets out a sharp gasp. "Uh, about that."

I arch a brow at her. "About what?"

"Last night, I was feeling artistic. I missed you and…"

"What did you do?"

"I cut a heart in your grass." She chews on her bottom lip, worry dancing in her eyes.

"Show me," I growl.

Reluctantly, she slides out of the bed, my cum glistening

on her thigh as she slips away. My cock hardens right back up, the basest male part of me appreciating the view. I watch her round, bubbly butt jiggle as she walks over to my window. Following after her, I wait for her to lift the blinds. I cringe when I see the big brown heart in the middle of my perfect green lawn. Tufts of grass litter the ground around it. How did I not notice this earlier?

So much for winning lawn of the year this year.

That's okay, I won the girl instead.

"Oh, you're such a bad, bad girl," I growl, my erection pressing against her from behind.

She gasps, her palms flattening against the glass. "I should be punished," she chimes in a little eagerly.

I chuckle as I step back and palm her sweet ass. "I completely agree, baby. Completely."

Slap!

She squeals but offers me her ass again.

Slap!

"Will," she whines. "I shouldn't have done that. I'm sorry."

I laugh as I slap her bottom once more. "And miss out on this? I'm not."

Grabbing a handful of her fleshy ass, I pull on her with one hand and guide my rock-hard erection to where she still drips from my last release. I grip her hip as I drive into her. Her palms slap against the glass and her forehead bumps it.

"Bad girls have to get fucked against the window," I murmur against her hair before seeking out her ear.

She moans and tilts her head to the side to give me access. I bite on the outside of her ear as I slide my palm to one of her tits. My other hand slips to her clit. I fuck her against the window for all to see if they simply look up. Mr. Daniels has probably been waiting for this moment his whole life.

"You know you're not leaving this bedroom today," I growl. "Hell, I don't know if I'll ever let you leave."

My words hit their intended mark or maybe it's the way I pinch at her swollen clit. Either way, she comes sharply, her body shuddering in my grip. It feels good the way her cunt milks me. I slam against her hard enough that our skin makes a slapping sound that rivals the whippings I gave her just moments ago. Her forehead thunks the glass again. My balls seize up with pleasure. Quickly, I pull out and stroke my red, throbbing cock until I'm spurting my seed all over her ass that bears my handprint. Ropes of hot cum splatter against her flesh and I've never seen anything hotter in my entire goddamned life.

"Caveman," she says, chuckling before she turns to face me.

"Damn straight," I grunt.

Her squeals of delight, when I once again toss her over my shoulder, fill my soul.

I carry her into the bathroom and start the shower. She's a messy girl and as much as I'd love to keep her that way, she looks hungover and nothing kills a hangover like a big break-fast. And last I checked, IHOP doesn't allow cum-covered naked hotties.

The water heats up and I pull her under the spray with me. Her arms wrap around my waist and she stares up at me as if I'm her whole world too. I take the time to simply stare at her, my fingers running gently through her hair that's quickly becoming soaked from the spray.

It's on my tongue. All the things I want to say to her.

"I'm glad we made up," she says. "And I'm glad you're officially my boyfriend." She flashes me a silly grin that makes my heart pound harder in my chest.

"I'm glad too, babe."

My gaze bores into hers and I stare at her with the hope that she sees just how much she gets under my skin and lives there. The way emotion flickers in her eyes, I think she knows.

I love you, Lilith Hamilton.

And one day I'll have the nerve to tell you.

Chapter Sixteen

Lilith

Thursdays are for Dropping Bombs

"Hi, Mr. Daniels." I wave as I skip back over to my house. More like slow run, since we both slept through the alarm, this being the third time this week and now I have seventeen minutes to shower and be on my way to work. I keep telling Will we need to spend more nights at my house, because at least I have a better working alarm, but he refuses to leave his pink coffee maker. He also confesses that those few moments stolen are the ones he loves the most. And I get why. It's because he always does a sneak attack and wakes me up with his mouth, his tongue, his gigantic...heart. I know, I just laughed too. But most importantly, he says it's those extra moments that he enjoys holding me close, knowing I'm all his.

I do a little swirl and skip up my steps. I wave at the birds chirping on the hanging bird feeder and hum my way into my house and into the shower. I know, I sound like a real-life Cinderella singing and dancing my way to my very own happily ever after. But, as the story says, if the shoe fits.

This week has been like no other. Amazing. Unreal. Perfect. Pick a word, they all fit the bill when it comes to

Will. I sometimes stop and take a few moments to admire just how wonderful he is. How lucky I am to have him. He's proven over and over that he doesn't care about my background. He couldn't care less about money. He's proven he's not intimidated by my family and he's stated in many forms there's nothing that will stop him from wanting me.

And boy does he.

In those moments, I take him in. His smile, his nerdy black frames that turn me on like no other. The way he loves his psycho cat. I watch him in the morning when he sips his coffee and reads the paper, being so interested in the world around him. One would say he's a bit overdramatic about the rules of society. I would have said the same just a short month ago. But the way Will wants to make things better is actually inspiring.

He explained it wasn't him being anal, it was him wanting to keep others safe. That sometimes the ones who do the most harm don't realize their faults. How everyone needs someone looking out for them. He simply wanted to, in some way, pay it forward. I asked who his savior was and joked around on what he could have possibly done that was so naughty. I caught the quick expression change, but he said his grandma was his angel. He said his naughty confession was what he was about to do to me. That's when he tackled me and fucked me so hard, I forgot what we were even talking about.

Being apart while we're at work sucks. Not that I don't feel like he's with me, since he calls every morning on his way to work to smooth talk our listeners. On Monday, he called in telling our listeners about his weekend. Of course, everything he said had them eating out of the palm of his hand. I seriously thought Leon was going to start sending *him* a paycheck. When he called on Tuesday, he asked our listeners how women felt about being serenaded to. Our polls said that ninety-two percent would fall head over heels for a guy who sang to her. So, come Wednesday, when he called to thank the listeners, he went on to say how he came home and made his neighbor caccavelle alla sorrentina, a homemade Italian pasta dish, with shredded parmesan and fresh tomato basil sauce. He told them how he sang an Italian love song to her while they ate under the moonlight. I laughed the entire time because he made me steak.

Him and his goddamn steak.

It's now Thursday, which I normally have off, but we have an upcoming band in for an interview, and D and I have to take them out afterward and show them a good time. I'm running through my house while undressing, knowing every second counts. I make it to my shower and turn the water on hot, when two hands grab me, and I scream bloody murder.

"Jesus, it's just me." Will laughs, holding me.

"What the hell? You almost gave me a heart attack! Why are you here? You're just as late!"

He seems not to care. He starts undressing and once we're both fully naked, he climbs into my shower with me.

"Will, we're both gonna be late," I say as the warm water hits my back. His hands are up my ribcage, one disappearing behind me and grabbing my butt cheek.

"Maybe I want you to be late. Maybe they'll fire you and you don't have to dangle this hot body in front of rockers when you're already taken."

I laugh against his lips that are now on mine, kissing me. I forget I have only thirteen minutes until I need to be speeding like a crazy person to work as I allow him to press my back against the cool tile and grind his yummy hard dick against my clit.

"I have to. It's my job. Plus, they're harmless. I was told they all have wives."

He presses me harder against the tile, maneuvering himself so he's right at my entrance. "I don't give a fuck about their wives. This pussy is mine and only mine. I don't even want them fantasizing about it." He then pushes inside me, and all thoughts of work and the eleven-minute warning go out the window as I meow like a cat in heat during my entire shower orgasm.

"And there you have it, folks, Kev from Love Drug. Make sure to check 'em out tomorrow night at Mandarin's. They'll be playing a full set, along with some extra bootleg tracks." Daryl presses some sound effect drums and clicks off air just as I barrel through the door.

"I'm soooo sorry," I whisper, throwing myself into my seat. I wave at the band, who's already up and leaving.

"Shit, what'd I miss? Is Leon in? How much trouble am I in?" I throw my headphones on and turn to the clock to see we have thirty seconds before we're back on air.

"Lil, you are lucky I love your bunk ass. He called in. Blew a tire. I told him you were takin' a shit."

I scowl at him because ew!

"I'll take that look as a thank you. But, girl, you need to get your shit together. I ain't gonna keep covering for you. And this is the last time you blow me off. First it was for Taco Tuesday. I had to sit there and listen to Manny cry on my shoulder because he thinks you don't like him anymore.

Then yesterday for the bowling. I only joined that shit 'cause of you."

"I'm sorry. And thank you. I've just been…preoccupied lately."

"You mean too busy riding Mr. Wonka's big wonka?"

Daryl laughs as I pick up a pen and toss it across the desk.

"That's not it. Well, it is, but…shit, I was totally late today because I was riding the big wonka." Dammit. I really need to do better with self-control in the mornings.

The light starts flashing that we have five seconds.

Four.

Three.

Two.

"And rise and shine, Morristown. Thanks for listening. Your support earns us our paychecks," I chirp.

"And half-off drinks at Mandarin's tonight on Fifty-Ninth Street. That's where you can find Lil and me, along with Love Drug. Looks like everyone should be having a smooth commute today. Let's hit the lines and see how it is out there. Hello, caller, you're on the air."

"Hey, Big D. It's Mr. Wonka."

Daryl's eyebrows go up at me, and I silently threaten to throw another pen at his head.

"Morning, Mr. Wonka. What updates you got for us today?" I shake my head but tune in to him because I'm also curious what stunt he's gonna pull today.

"Big D, I was hoping I could get personal with you. I'm having a problem with my cat. Can we talk pets for a moment?"

Daryl's brows go up, confused, whereas mine crinkle. "Wonka, I'm not sure listeners want to hear about your feline problems," I say, secretly telling him he better not dare.

"I don't know. I feel like they could really help me out. You see, I have this cat. She's a feisty little thing. Meowed all morning in the shower." Oh, here we go. "So needy. Always wanting to be petted."

Oh, give me a break. "Sounds like you need to get your cat in check, dawg," Daryl says, laughing as he slowly catches on.

"I agree. You see, she loves going out. Little thing loves to roam around at night. Makes me a not-so-happy owner. I get jealous. I don't want anyone else petting my kitty."

Daryl laughs more and begins to play meowing sound effects. "Maybe you need to be sterner with her. Have you thought about caging her?"

Give me a flipping—

"I have actually. I've spanked her many times, telling her to stay inside. Her favorite place is my bedroom anyway. No need to ever leave. But she just doesn't listen."

"Wonka, maybe you should trust that your cat's simply going out and being a cat. She always comes home to you."

"You think? It's just that, I think she's in heat. This morning, while in the shower, she scratched down my back pretty good."

"I did—I mean, I doubt that. Cats don't even like water." Shit, I almost busted myself out.

"Well, this cat, she's different. She has this spunk about her. She's not like any other cat. And I just want to keep her all for myself."

My heart warms at his comment. My annoyance at his daily stunt turns into softness from his sweet underlying comment.

"Well, Wonka, maybe you should just wait your sweet rump at home for your cat to come back and if you're lucky maybe she'll purr in such delight it wakes the neighbors."

Will laughs. "I hope so, because she sure is something special."

"I will! Rock on brother man!" I laugh and point to Kev as I exit Mandarin's and allow the door behind me to slam. I look at my phone in search of the Uber app. I didn't plan on drinking enough not to drive, but damn those rockers sure put the pressure on. Not to mention, Betsy the bartender, makes a mean dirty martini. I'm digging through my purse for my keys to make sure my car's locked when my phone buzzes. It's a text from Will.

Wonka: When are you coming home? I have a cage and a whip ready to do some major spanking to that pussy.

I blush like a school girl at his racy text. Never in a million years would I have pegged my nerdy, anal neighbor as a dirty talker. I shoot off a quick text back.

Me: I'm coming right meow. Waiting on Uber.

My stomach does a bunch of summersaults at what I can possibly expect once I get home. I'm crossing my fingers and toes that Will is super strict and disciplines this kitty for being so late. My thighs squeeze together in anticipation. I check my phone to see where my driver is, when a call comes through. It's my father.

Not sure why he's calling this late, but I decide to ignore it. Going back to my app, I wait for it to update, when my father calls in again.

"Seriously, what gives?" I swipe the call and answer.

"Hello, dearest Father, to what do I owe the pleasure of this call?"

"Lilith."

"That's my name. Don't wear it out or you're gonna have to buy a new one!" Okay, maybe I had one too many of Betsy's martinis.

"Lilith, good God. Have you been drinking?"

That's an understatement.

"I was at a club social, Daddy. Is there a reason you're ringing me at such an hour?"

"Yes. I need you to come to the house."

"Great, I'll see if I can find some time this weekend—"

"Now, Lilith. It cannot wait."

I pull my phone away to look at the time. It's almost midnight. "Daddy, it's a little late. Plus, I can't drive. I'll come by—"

"There's a car coming to pick you up." And just like that a black town car pulls around the corner.

"What? How did you know where I was?"

"For God's sake, Lilith, you're my daughter. I always know where you are."

That comment drowns the good mood I was in. "Well, I also told you now's not a good time. I'll come by when I—"

"Get in the car, Lilith. You will regret it if you don't." And then the line goes dead.

The car pulls up to me and a gentleman gets out and opens the door for me. With a huge scowl on my face, I give in and get in. I know I could fight my father on this, but maybe it's better to just get it over with. Tell him he has no control over me and be done.

Since the dinner, I've had a lot of time to think. And being with Will, it's made me realize my father truly has no hold over me. I don't need his money or his name. I would be just as happy living off ramen and Will's smile just as much as if I were swimming in riches. The thing I realized is you can't put a price tag on what Will and I have. Because it truly is priceless.

I'm done letting my father control me. He can take everything away from me, and I'm willing to accept that. If he turns his back on his only daughter, then that's something he'll also have to live with. But me? I'll still have Will. I'll still be myself. I'll have my freedom.

I spend the drive practicing the speech I'm going to give my father. I send off a text to Will, telling him his naughty kitty is going to be late, that I must make a pit stop, but be ready. I am ready to be punished for my tardiness.

By the time we reach my parents' estate, my buzz has worn off and I just want to get this over with so I can head back home to Will. Simmons, our butler, greets me as I hop up the royal palace stairs in front of their home.

"What's shakin' Simmons?" I ask and high five him. Simmons is old and on the verge of retiring, but my parents swear he has a lifetime left in him.

"Not much, Miss Lilith. I am to let you know your father is in his study."

"Thanks!" I say as I walk through the marble-floored foyer and down the hall to my father's study.

The door is open a crack. I knock and open it, walking in to find him at his desk.

"Let's make this fast. I have plans. Actually, I'll start. You are not going to control—"

"Sit down," my father snaps, cutting off my rehearsed speech.

"No. I'm not going to be your little—"

"SIT. DOWN," he barks and down I go.

"Why am I here, Daddy? This could have waited until normal hours. And to be honest, I don't care what you have to say. I've made up my mind. This is my life. I'm staying in Morristown. I'm staying with Will."

My father stands, his large frame dominating the room. "I always knew obedience was something you lacked. All the tutors in the world couldn't teach you proper manners."

I feel like he just slapped me with his insult. I open my mouth to argue back, but his hand goes up.

"I've tried to give you everything you wanted. I allowed this silly sabbatical to happen. But it's gone too far. You think you know everything. So smart, my naïve daughter."

That's it. I rise hastily from my chair. "You know what? No, I don't have to sit through this."

That's when he tosses a folder at me. It slings across his desk and I catch it before it slides off and the insides spill to the ground. "What is this?"

"It's why you're done playing this little game. It's why you're not mature enough to keep this family name clean. You think I've worked this hard for you to lose your way and tarnish the Hamilton name?"

"What are you talking about? I've done nothing to tarnish this family! This isn't about me. This is about you and your obsession to control people. I'm not some employee you can boss around. I'm your daughter."

"Yes, and I'm the only one it seems who has your best interests in mind."

"Oh, and how is that so?"

"Open the folder."

I forgot I was even holding it. With a huff, I pull my searing eyes away from my father and open the file. Confused about what I'm seeing at first, it takes a moment or two for it to register.

"Wha—what is all this?"

"Information I'm sure your little boyfriend failed to mention."

I flip through the corresponding documents. They seem to be investigation findings from a private investigator.

Investigation Report

Consensus: Report states, twenty-year-old William A. Grant was arrested for suspicion of arson after setting fire to the home of Barbara Grant. Grant was booked for arson, along with being under the influence of illegal drugs. Grant has a long list of priors, all drug related.

"What is this? Where did you get this?" I flip the page to another report. These aren't official reports but those compiled by a private investigator. I question the validity but keep reading.

William Grant was under the influence of illegal drugs. His system was positive for marijuana and Vicodin. He was admitted for a thirty-day treatment as ordered by the court.

"This isn't true."

"Reports don't lie, Lilith."

"Well, you could have easily forged these! They're not official reports, Daddy. You would do anything to get me home and married off under your control."

"That might be true, but it doesn't change the fact your boyfriend is a criminal—"

"He's not a criminal! Why are you doing this?" I tear my eyes away from the horrible things I'm reading and stare back at my father.

"Because you are blinded, child. You are seeing a man who is not a good man. He's going to ruin you and this family's good name."

"He is a good man, Daddy."

"Then keep reading."

My heart plummets at those three words. Will mentioned he used to be a bad boy. A loser. But this was not what I had imagined when he used those words. I turn the page again to see an article from the *Morristown Gazette* with a photo attached. It's of Will and a woman. The woman from Sunday. My heart plummets even more.

"Gerald and Caroline Campbell of Morristown, New Jersey, are pleased to announce the engagement of their daughter, Presley Elizabeth Campbell, to William A. Grant, grandson of Barbara Grant of Morristown. William A. Grant is an internal bank auditor at Huffington Bank and Trust. An October wedding is planned."

"He was engaged?"

"I assume he never mentioned that one."

I lift my eyes and give my father a hateful stare. "This doesn't mean anything. His past is his past. It has no bearing on the present."

"Flip to the next page, Lilith."

No, I don't want to. My father holds my stare until I buckle and flip the page. It's another sketchy report from the investigator. The title, in bold, reads:

Wedding Called off Due to Groom's Scam

Information leading up to the Campbell/Grant wedding provides detailed evidence that the relationship was a farce and the groom was in it for the money. Sources close to Grant confess he admitted he searched out the bride, knowing the extent of wealth he would gain by marrying the young debutante.

As I read through the report, tears start to fall down my face. Every word that's printed sends an aching pain to my chest. "Where did you get this?" I lift my gaze to my father. He doesn't respond. Instead, he picks up his crystal glass filled with bourbon and takes a hefty sip. "I asked you where you got this." My hands shake as emotions threaten to overtake me.

"It doesn't matter. What matters is his intentions are obvious. This is why I'm so protective over you. So people like him don't try and fool you in an effort to marry into your money."

No.

"He didn't even know I came from money. He didn't know."

"How so? Are you trying to tell me that him being in the banking business, he never heard of Hamilton Investments? Never saw a photo of *my* daughter in the many Wall Street magazines? For God's sake, Lilith, I own the bank he works for."

That shocks me. "You do?"

"I do. It would be simple to put the pieces together. I haven't gotten to where I am today without my keen eye for detecting potential fraud."

I don't want to believe it.

But how do I ignore it? I can't. I asked Will to be honest with me, and even after our talk, my instincts still told me he was hiding something. But I never thought it would be this. I never thought…

"I had your room made up. I'll have Simmons send for your things first thing in the morning."

That's when I snap. "You know what, congratulations. You won this one. You proved me wrong. Apparently, no matter how far I run from this life, there will always be someone wanting me for only my last name. But I'm not coming home. This might change who I trust, but it doesn't change the fact I'm done being a prisoner under your spell."

I toss the folder onto my father's mahogany desk and turn around to leave. I walk out of his study, his booming voice demanding I come back, but his threats fall on deaf ears. I can't stay a second longer in this house.

I ask Simmons to give me a ride home, which he thankfully obliges without question. The entire ride home I fight the sickness that's swirling in my stomach. I can't believe I was ready to say those three magical words, and it was just a scam. Will knew I had money all along. He knew he was winning me over. It explains why he was so understanding when he found out who I really was. The amount I was truly worth.

My head is pounding, my mind screaming as I rehash every single moment we've spent together. Every time I felt this pull between us. This feeling that was so unexplainable, it was just me being naïve. None of it was real. And I was a fool.

By the time Simmons pulls up to my house, my eyes are bloodshot and swollen. My temper is boiling, and my heart is fucking shattered. I get out of the town car, thank Simmons, and walk up to my house.

Will's door opens. "Here, kitty kitty. Come over and I may have some cream for you."

His joke makes me cry again. I'm torn between running inside my house or going to his and blowing up. I just don't know if I can trust myself right now.

"Hey, baby, come on. What are you doing just standing there?"

Him calling me baby does it. It's blow up time. I storm up to his front porch. I take the steps two at a time until I'm in his face. That's when I raise my hand and slap him hard across the face.

His shock is immediate.

I don't allow it to register, I raise my hand and slap him again. When I go for a third, he grabs my wrist tightly, stopping me.

"I'm not sure where this is coming from, but I'm going to ask that you stop fucking slapping me." His voice is low and furious.

"You thought you could play me, huh?" I struggle to get my hand free, but he only grips it tighter.

"I have no idea what you're talking about, but I'm not *playing* you. Where have you been?"

I pull at my arm again, with no luck. "Screw you. None of your business. Let me go."

"Not until you tell me what the hell is going on."

"Let's just say I know everything. Your past, your *fiancée.*" I feel him jolt at the word. "Yeah, I know everything. Even your intentions with me!" I raise my other hand, taking a swing at him, but he blocks me. I fight in his arms, until he can't keep hold of me and lets me go.

"Who told you?"

"So, you're not even going to deny it? You bastard." My face is soaked with tears. I'm struggling to catch my breath. He doesn't even have an argument, which tells me all of it is true. "You know, my father might be a lot of things, but one thing he's not is an idiot. He did his research on you. Showed me the person you used to be. How you were engaged. How she found out you were scamming her for her money! Man, I bet you thought you hit the jackpot with me, didn't you?"

"What are you talking about? Yes, I was engaged. Yes, I

have a past. I wasn't hiding it, but I never sought anyone out for money. Presley and I—"

"Ahhh, Presley. The nobody who was at your house last weekend. Did you invite her over after our fight? Hope to rekindle old flames? Get into her pockets like you were gonna do mine?"

"Jesus Christ, what are you talking about? I'm not getting into anyone's pockets. I didn't even know—"

"Bullshit! You knew! How could you not! Hamilton Investments owns Huffington Bank and Trust! You knew!"

"Lil, I swear—"

He comes at me, but I slap his hands away. "Stay away from me. I'm done. We're done."

"We're not done. Whatever your father must have told you are lies. Just let me explain."

"Yeah, too late, Will. Now that my father opened my eyes and dropped the bomb on your scheming plan, you think I'm gonna just listen to whatever it is you have to say?"

"Yes, dammit, because it'll be the truth and not the lies your deceiving father fed you."

I take a step toward him. "Don't talk about my father. At least he cares enough to tell me the truth."

"Lil, please."

"No. Screw you, Will. Screw you. Stay the fuck away from me."

And with that I run down his porch steps, across the lawn, and throw myself inside my house. I hear him calling my name, but I don't look back at the destruction.

Chapter Seventeen

Will

Thursdays are for Breakups—
You Know What? Fuck that.

She knows.

Goddammit, she knows.

Well, half of it. Some of it. Part of it. Definitely not all of it.

But what she doesn't know is that most of it is bullshit. Her meddling father is an idiot if he thinks he can weave lies and half-truths mixed into my actual past in an effort to run me off.

You know what? Fuck that.

Fuck him.

Fuck the forces trying to drive Lilith and me apart.

Unlike last time where I let her go, this time I'll be damned if I let the girl get away. Slamming the door behind me, I trot after her. When I get to her door, it's locked. She was too upset to hide the key, so I lift the gnome and steal it. I let myself inside and close the door behind me.

Every light is on, but it's quiet.

Too quiet.

Quietly, I walk down her hallway and prowl to her bedroom. When I cross over her threshold, my heart sinks.

My sweet, beautiful Lilith. Crying. Her body shakes as she sobs face down on her bed. An ache forms in my chest and I know I'll do anything to fix it. To fix her. To fucking fix us. Anything.

I just need to make her listen.

Kicking off my shoes along the way, I walk over to the bed. When the mattress moves with my weight, she stiffens.

"Leave," she chokes out.

"No."

I climb on top of her and rest my weight on her, my nose nuzzling in her hair. She cries and I simply hold her, pressing kisses to her skull. We don't fight or scream or argue. I just nonverbally try to communicate how much I love her until she's ready to listen to what I have to say.

"She's nobody to me," I say after a while.

Her body tenses. "So you've said."

"The stuff you told me outside earlier, only part of it was true, Lilith."

"*All* of it was horrible," she whispers.

Wincing, I close my eyes. It's now or never. "When I was twenty, I accidentally set fire to my grandma's house. I was high on enough prescription drugs to keep a horse tranquilized. Passed out with a cigarette in my hand and caught my childhood home on fire." I let out a heavy sigh. "Grandma was at work. By the time I awoke, flames had engulfed half of my room. I was so fucked up, I could barely get out of my room, much less try to stop it. From the neighbor's driveway, I watched all of our memories burn to the ground."

The flames. The smoke. The sirens.

Nothing compares to the loud, ugly sobs that came from my grandma.

And still yet, she loved me. My grandma advocated for me.

"I was arrested on suspicion of arson since I was under the influence, but the fire marshal later determined the fire was set by a cigarette and deemed it an accident," I reveal softly. My fingers run along the outside of her arm. Goose bumps rise at my touch. "Grandma obviously didn't press charges and helped bail me out of a shit-ton of trouble, but she was adamant I sought treatment after that. I got cleaned up and vowed I'd never be so reckless with my life again. Reckless means hurting those around you. I'd been spiraling, Lilith. The fire and subsequent forced rehab is what made me stop spinning. Finally, I had the wakeup call I needed."

She's quiet and not forcing me out of her house, so I continue.

"Every time I go to Grandma's new place, I'm overcome with guilt. No amount of time can pass where I don't hear those gut-wrenching sobs playing over and over again in my head. Photos of me as a baby. Memories of my deceased parents and grandfather. Every single memory she and I ever had was gone." I inhale her hair and rub my thumb across her arm. "But I would never hurt my grandma on purpose."

"I don't see how this has anything to do with *her*. The *nobody*," she bites out, her voice cold.

Lifting up, I push Lilith onto her back and then pin her again with my body. I need to see her pretty brown eyes and pouty lips. Tonight, her eyes are bloodshot and her nose is pink from crying. It breaks my fucking heart seeing her like this.

"After the fire, I was so overcome with grief and self-loathing that I took a different path. I got into college and busted my ass with my studies while working part-time.

Gave every extra penny to Grandma in an effort to help her out. Eventually, I got my finance degree. I worked many jobs throughout the years and then I was able to work for a bank. Despite my past, they hired me because my work history proved I was really good at what I do." I run my fingers along her jaw and furl my eyes together. "I have an obsessive personality."

"No, not *you*," she says dryly, a small sliver of the usual Lilith shining through.

I hold onto that tiny bit of hope and smile. "When I put my mind to something, I put one hundred percent of my focus on it. Drugs back in the day. Education when I straightened my shit up. Terrorizing the hot neighbor last year. Then, loving her."

Tears shine in her eyes and she looks away. "And the *nobody*?"

Guilt surges through me, but I come out with it. "I was so dead set on proving to everyone I was a decent human being I started dating Presley. Someone smart and pretty and influential. I met her at a bank function. She was the daughter of one of the investors. We hit it off because she was everything I wanted to be. She was...so put together." Flashes of Presley with her sleek blond hair and plastic smile fill my head.

"Great, wonderful. She was so amazing," Lilith snaps. "Then what?"

I bite back a smile at her jealousy, even now. "I did everything to make her happy. She was—or so I thought—the key to this ultimate happiness. I was just sure I'd marry her and we'd live happily ever after. That Grandma would finally be proud of the man I'd become." I frown and close my eyes. "That maybe she'd forgive me."

"Your grandma loves you," she whispers.

I blink my eyes open. "But I ruined her life."

Her palm strokes along my cheek and I lean into her touch. For a moment, we savor the peaceful pause. Then, she slaps me hard enough to startle me to bring me back to our argument. "And then?"

"I obsessed and obsessed like you know I do. Presley said I made her uncomfortable to be around. That I was too anal." I clench my jaw. "I just wanted everything to be perfect." Letting out a heavy sigh, I say, "But it wasn't perfect. My life was always missing something."

"Money," she blurts out.

"What? No." I run my thumb over her swollen bottom lip. "You, Lilith."

"Because I have money."

"I don't give a fuck about your money," I growl. "My life was missing you. In my hunt for perfection, I realized it wasn't what I wanted. What I wanted, what led me to all the shit I'd done in the past, was the desire to be happy. Always reaching and never grasping. Then one day, I had you. This beautiful, sweet, vibrant hell cat in my arms." I run my fingers through her hair. "I just wanted to pull you into my arms and never let go. Once I realized perfection was bullshit but happiness was real, I knew I had that chance at it with you. I finally felt I had a life worth living."

"Why was she here?" she asks, her bottom lip quivering.

"To tell me she was pregnant."

"You asshole!" she screeches, wiggling in my arms.

Grabbing her wrists, I press them into the mattress and lean my forehead against hers. "Not *my* baby, Lilith. Some guy. She broke up with me ages ago and was seeing one of her father's friends. He knocked her up and apparently decided his marriage to his wife was more important than dropping everything to take care of his mistress. I think she thought maybe we'd rekindle what we had."

"But…" she urges me on.

"But I didn't give in because I'm no longer her perfect fiancé. I'm Lilith Hamilton's imperfect sonofabitch boyfriend who makes her cry on the regular, but desperately wishes she wouldn't." I press my lips to hers and she doesn't try to get away. "I'm yours, Lil. Fucked up and flawed. My past sucks. I've made a bunch of mistakes I'm embarrassed of. I just wanted to push them away and focus on my future. To focus on me and you because, baby, we aren't ugly. Together we're something pretty fucking amazing."

I tangle my fingers in her hair and kiss her deeply. Her tongue is tentative at first, but then she kisses me back as though she needs me as much as I need her. We make out like a couple of teenagers until we're panting and I'm hard as a fucking rock.

"So I'm just some rando you got hot for? You didn't seek me out like Daddy says because of my money?" she asks, her brows furling together.

"Just some rando I wanted to hate but then wanted to fuck," I say with a crooked grin.

She laughs and it's the cutest sound ever. "I think that was supposed to be a compliment, Wonka. You really are imperfect."

Smirking, I agree, "Most definitely."

"I just wish you had told me," she says finally, letting out a ragged breath.

"I'm ashamed of my past," I admit. "What guy wants to admit to the woman he loves that he was a major fuck-up who made a bunch of horrible mistakes?"

"Loves?" She quirks up a brow in question.

"I love you, Lilith. I know it's early and irrational and probably another mistake on my laundry list of shit I do wrong, but I don't care. You're inside of me. I couldn't get you out if I tried."

"It's not a mistake," she murmurs. "I love you too. Even if you are a big idiot who should have just told me in the first place."

"I'm sorry. I just can't lose you. You mean too much to me."

"You're forgiven. And tomorrow, I'm going to tell Daddy to stop trying to invade my life. I'm a grown woman who can make her own"—she smirks at me—"mistakes."

I kiss her mouth before sliding off her. She lets out a squeal when I grab her thigh and drag her off the bed.

"Will!" she cries out when I hoist her over my shoulder. "What are you doing?"

"I'm taking you home."

One week later…

I can't stop thinking about the information I dug up on the computer earlier this morning and ponder what I should do with it. Maybe I don't do anything at all. He certainly doesn't deserve it. It's probably nothing. And yet…I can't ignore it.

Blame my obsessive personality.

Blame my confrontational nature.

Blame the powers that be who are dangling this in front of my face and luring me into the devil's den.

"He'll be with you in a moment," the receptionist says.

I've long gone over my lunch hour waiting on this prick, but now I'm fully invested. No backing out now. Finally, he emerges from his office and a man follows him out.

Tall. Arrogant. Regal.

But behind all that shit is Lilith's father.

And I need to do this.

"Mr. Grant," he says coldly. Then he smirks as he gestures to the man behind him. "Meet Lance Peterson."

Lance.

The Lance.

I size him up for a moment. Take in his comb-over and small stain on his tie. I note his size in comparison to mine. Shorter and less fit. After a moment, I realize he is not a threat to me. "Your reputation precedes you," I tell him.

He smiles, all bright and shiny veneers in his mouth. Money may not be able to buy you a steady hand at lunch or more hair, but it can sure buy you a fancy smile. "Good to meet you," he says as he extends his hand.

Feminine yet extremely hairy hand, I might add.

I accept his offering and when he squeezes me hard, a known power play done between rivaling businessmen, I politely crush him in my grip. His face turns red and he quickly jerks his hand away.

"I'll see you and your parents later for dinner," Bart tells him before waving him away. "Please, do come in."

I follow the man into his expansive office and take the offered seat. When he sits at his desk, he steeples his fingers and glares at me.

"Enough with the pretenses, William," he snarls. "Why are you here? To gloat that you somehow conned my Lilith into believing your lies?"

Shaking my head, I bite back the angry words I want to

say to him. "Everything I told her was the truth. I love Lilith. And because I love her, I'm here today to talk."

"You'll never be a Lance Peterson, so you may as well not try. I'm not here to make peace," he grumbles.

God, he's fucking impossible.

With a huff, I pull out the folded papers from my pocket and toss them at him. "Here. Read those."

He narrows his eyes at me but picks up the papers as if they carry the plague. Then, he unfolds them and begins reading. With each second that passes, his face turns redder and redder. "What is the meaning of this?" he demands.

"Like I told you at dinner that night, I make it *my* business to dig too, Mr. Hamilton. And after that night, I just couldn't let it go. It's my future legacy after all," I taunt, enjoying the way his vein in his neck bulges. "But all that aside, it needs to be addressed. You have the information right there. Now follow those leads."

"Get out," he hisses.

"I do this for a living," I remind him.

"Get the hell out of my office or I'll send security after you."

Rising, I hold my palms up. "Maybe if you take five minutes from trying to ruin your daughter's life, you could take a nice clear look at your own." The papers crumple in his fist and I shrug. "Suit yourself, old man. Do what you want with it but do hear what I have to say," I tell him lowly. "Lilith is my girlfriend. I fucking love her. And there's not a goddamned thing you can do about it. So stay the hell out of our lives."

Fuck, that felt good.

"You'll pay for this, Grant!" he bellows after me. "Just wait! Lilith will eventually leave you high and dry. It's what she does. And Lance Peterson will be waiting with open arms. Mark my words, son."

I let him know exactly what I think about his words...

I flip off the great Bart Hamilton.

Fuck, that felt *really* good.

Chapter Eighteen

Lilith

Saturdays are for Double the Pussy Shaving

Two weeks later...

Too girly. *Toss.*

Too edgy. *Toss.*

Possibly too see-through. *Toss, toss. Toss...*

I toss outfit after outfit out of my closet and onto the mound of clothes that all scream date night rejects. Because tonight, I have a very important date.

My first problem is, I have nothing to wear.

While on air this week, Will called in asking for suggestions on the perfect date. He wanted to take his neighbor on a date she would never forget.

And so, it started.

The week-long polls, call-ins, emails, and surveys on the creation of the perfect date for Wonka and his *neighbor*. The candle-light dinner along a waterfront, to the rock concert. The yacht rental, to blowing his savings on a sporadic trip to Paris. There was no doubt I egged on anything sporadic, since my neighbor was *anything* but.

The second problem being, I haven't been able to get into my bathroom to get ready.

And that problem is fluffy and has very sharp claws.

Will had to leave on an impromptu bank training trip and asked if I could take his sweet cat while he was away. *She doesn't like to be alone, he says. She's sensitive like that, he says.* She stared me down with those devil cat eyes as I thought, hell fucking no way was I going to take Satan's ball of fur. The words 'no fucking thanks' were just about to fall off my tongue when I then witnessed him gaze at his cat and smile. Like he was looking at the sweetest, most precious little kitty he's ever known. And his love for that psycho feline had me saying yes, I'd love to. I swear I saw that evil cat smile at me.

So, when Will dropped her off and gave me the best goodbye kiss known to man, the second that door closed, it was on. That furry shit attacked me. It's a good thing I've got moves, because if I wasn't so quick to dodge her, I would have had her claws stuck to my face. I thought she would go hide under a chair and stay clear of me for the next two days, but nope. It's like she was reading my every move. I wanted to go watch some TV? She jumped on the couch and dared me to try and sit down. I went into the kitchen to drink myself into becoming a cat lover, and she was pouncing past me and lying in front of my pantry. I literally slept on my couch last night because that fuzzball was on my bed!

I woke up this morning sore and crabby. While Satan was still getting her beauty rest I was able to make some coffee. I sat with my cup behind the door and waited for her to come out. The moment I saw her tail sashay past me, I jumped into my room and shut the door.

Winner.

But now as I shuffle through all my clothes and realize I have nothing to wear, I also realize I'm stuck in here. I take a time out and sit on a pile of clothes and sip my coffee. I think about how it doesn't matter what I have on, because that's not who Will is. He's not superficial, or judgmental. I'm sure I can wear a paper bag and he would still see beauty. At least he better. I laugh when I hear my phone vibrating on my nightstand. I get up to retrieve it and see a paw clawing under the door as I pass by.

"Not a chance, fur freak." I'm tempted to kick the door just to startle her away, but I have to have some control. I am the adult here. The *human* adult. I grab my phone and just like the last five missed calls, it's my father ringing through. Not one of those calls apologizing for his deceiving ways. He may think he's doing what's best for me, but there's no excuse for what he did. Lying to me. The pain he caused, allowing me to think Will had been deceitful to me this whole time. I miss the call on purpose and walk back to my closet. It goes off again. I groan, knowing he's probably not going to stop. I head back and grab it, swiping to answer.

"What do you want?"

"Manners, Lilith," he scolds.

"Really, Daddy? You want to talk about manners? How about we talk about lying? Deceiving people and trying to ruin people's lives? Let's talk about that?"

"Lilith, I'm just trying to protect you. I don't want you to get hurt. You deserve to be cared for. Can this man care for you? Is he well educated enough to hold a job? Excel? What kind of life do you think William Grant truly can offer you?"

My anger spikes. The coffee in my mug vibrates as my hands begin to shake. "How dare you! William Grant is the best man I've ever met. And I don't care if he works on the street selling hot dogs. It's not about money, Daddy. It's about someone who loves me."

"Lance loves you."

"FUCK LANCE!" I yell.

"You watch your tone with me, child. I am still your father."

"No, you're a man who just wants to control me. You don't care about my happiness. You care about what image I'll portray. I'm not like you. I don't need all those fancy things to be happy or to feel established. I need nothing from you."

"I would watch what you wish for."

"Oh yeah? What possibly can you do now? You've already tried. And it didn't work. Do your worst. I'm done being a prisoner under your hold. Bye, Daddy."

I hang up and throw my phone.

My hands are shaking so bad, I'm forced to put my coffee mug down before it all splashes out. I am done with him trying to control me. He may think he knows best, but this is my life. And I chose Will. I decided I'll have plenty of time on Sunday, before Will gets home, to finish prepping. I grab my phone and send a text to D telling him I need a full day of heavy drinking and to meet me at Manny's. Then I proceed to climb out my window, instead of facing my furry enemy.

"Girl, are you sure you're okay?"

"Yez, just yep, gonna go sleep." I climb out of D's car and almost eat the ground. I hear him laughing and I bounce back up.

"I'm okay!" I chirp, laughing at myself. I wave him off

and stumble up my steps. I jam my hands in my purse in search of my keys. "Where areee you?" I sing as I find them deep down in the side pocket. I unlock my door and as I turn to wave at Daryl, I hear it.

The hiss.

Fuck me.

I forgot about Björk.

I hurry up and shut my front door. "I need a plan B." I say to my drunk self. I know I can climb back through my bedroom window, but it was a bit of a fall, so I'm not sure I have it in me to scale the side of my house to get back in. I head out back and check the sliding glass door, but it's locked.

"Dammit," I mumble, eyeing the lawn chair. "Well, it can't be as bad as the couch."

My phone buzzes in my pocket and I reach for it.

Wonka: Good news. I'm catching an earlier flight. I'll be home around nine tonight. Miss you. Can't wait to see you.

"Shit." I look at the time. "Shit!" It's almost eight. I ditched all my prepping chores because I thought I had time to finish them all tomorrow. If Will's coming home tonight, that means...

"Shit!"

I need to shower, paint my nails, shave a long list of body parts, and I'm literally seeing two of everything right now. Mainly, I need to get into my damn house without being clawed to death. I peek through the sliding glass door. Björk is in the kitchen staring right at me.

I do what comes naturally and give her the bird.

Sadly, it doesn't seem to faze her.

Why am I even out here? She's a damn cat. That's my

house. I'm the boss.

"Listen, he can love us both. There's no reason for us to be fighting like this. Can't we just be cordial?" I say through the glass. I watch as she jumps onto my counter and takes a squat. "You're gonna have to learn to like me. I plan on marrying your daddy one day and I'm gonna be your step mommy. It's best we settle our differences now." The mental image of one day walking down the aisle to Will gets my heart beating faster. He makes me so happy and I know I make him happy too. The mental thought that he'd probably ask me to make Björk a bridesmaid has me rolling my eyes and groaning.

"Cat, I don't care if you like me. Your daddy loves me. So you're gonna deal with it!" I raise my voice, stabbing my finger into the glass.

That's when Björk takes her paw and swipes the bowl of fruit off my counter.

"Oh no, you *didn't*." I gasp as I watch the bowl shatter and oranges and apples roll all over my kitchen floor. "You know what? That is it! We are sooo getting a dog." I storm off my back patio and head to the front. I grab the hose and turn it on. I unlock my door and the second she comes at me, I press the nozzle.

I watch as the water smacks Björk right in the nose. She hisses as I soak her, but not enough, in my opinion, before she takes off down the hall. I drop the hose, feeling awesome. Not about how I just soaked my living room like a drunk idiot, but more because I got that damn cat. I hurry and shut the door behind me before cautiously making my way down the hallway. I just need to get to my room and I'm golden. I can hide out there and get ready until Will gets home and he can remove her from my house.

I see a small patch of fur in between my washer and dryer in the laundry room and quickly shut the door, locking her in. "Bam! Ha. I win." I glance at my watch again and realize it's now a quarter past eight. My time is dwindling fast and I have *a lot* to do. I run to my room, slipping on the water on the floor, and make it into my bathroom. I set out a nice red laced bra with matching panties. I toss my clothes off and remember I need to shave. Like bad.

"This is the job of heavy duty machinery," I say, reaching in my drawer for my electric razor. Being inebriated, I come up with this great idea of how to surprise Will. Naked, I try and steady myself by lifting my leg onto the counter to get a good look at my goods. I'm not a designer by any means but how hard can it be to shave a W? I can't stop chuckling as I turn it on and start on my project.

"He's going to love this when he sees it." I giggle, losing my balance, and my foot falls off the counter. I grab at the wall, preventing myself from falling. "Holy shit," I cuss, almost swiping off a lip with my razor. "You got this." I lift my leg again and make another attempt. I get the first outline of the W and I feel good about it. As I go back up to form the middle part, I hear it.

The hiss.

How the hell did she get out of the laundry room?

I should have blocked the door because this isn't the first time she's managed to open a closed door in my house.

You have to be smarter than that psycho cat, Lil!

Everything after that happens so fast. The claws on my butt. My quick turn to fight. The sounds of my razor sawing away at hair. Not mine. By the time I get control of my balance and eyesight, my attacker is gone. But what is left behind is a huge chunk of fur.

Oh shit.

Double oh shit.

"He's going to kill me."

A jiggle comes from the front door. Oh my God! I look at my watch. *No no no...*

"Lil?" Will's voice sounds throughout the house. Sheer panic strikes me as I run out of the bathroom into my bedroom. "Babe, where are you at?"

I snap out of it in time to throw myself into a pair of solid underwear so he doesn't notice the botched shave job. I don't know how I'm gonna hide the other botched job.

"Lilith?"

"Coming!" I shout, looking under my bed, then in my closet with no luck. For all I know she ran straight to him to show him my handiwork. I'm so dead. I can see it now. He's gonna ask me what in the hell is going on and when I reply with just having a good ol' pussy shaving party with his cat, he's gonna break it off with me and take his cat and never talk to me again.

I grab a shirt and throw it on and run down the hallway. I slide half the way and greet him in the living room. He's taking in the water in my living room while I nonchalantly look for his cat.

"What the hell happened?"

"Oh, this? I dropped a glass of water."

He brings his eyes to mine. Yeah, those don't look like they believe me. "Riiiight. Where's—"

I jump on him.

"Whoa." He gasps as I throw myself into his arms, cutting his unnecessary question. He tries to keep upright and slips on the water, taking us both down to the ground. The fall is less painful than the question I almost had to answer. I waste no time and sit up and toss off my shirt.

"I've really missed you," I say, going down and kissing him like an animal in heat.

"I've missed you too. Where's—"

Dammit, stop asking.

I slam my lips back onto his. I kiss him, feeling the smile breach his lips. His hands squeeze my ass and he grinds himself into me.

"Have sex with me right now. Anything you want. Take me and rough me up. No more talking." Come on...I need to distract his mind to the right pussy.

I get a promising growl and before I know it, I'm being flipped and off go my panties.

Shit.

"Hey, Will?" I ask, still lying on the floor, both of us trying to catch our breaths.

"Yeah, baby?"

I sit up. "You know that money has never been important to me, right?"

That gets his attention. He sits up with me. "Of course, I know that. What's bringing this up? Is it your dad? Did he do something else?" I can tell he's starting to get worked up. Any time I bring up my father, it puts Will on edge. Rightfully so after the last incident.

"No, well, kind of. My father may never give up trying to control me. And when he does, it might be him cutting me off completely. I'm okay with it. I just want you to know. That it's just me—"

He kisses me, shutting me up. He pulls away once air

is a requirement and locks eyes with me. "I wouldn't care if you were homeless. I'd still love you. I want you for what's in here." He taps over my heart. "And if you keep being this amazing, down to earth girl whom I love like crazy, then there's nothing that will change how I feel about you."

"Promise?"

He reaches up and caresses my cheek. "I promise you. What's brought this up?"

I stall, not knowing how to really respond. There is this part of me that may continue to worry that where I came from will always define me. People will see me as a ticket to greater things. "Nothing. But I do need to tell you something. And you may be mad and not think I'm so amazing after I tell you."

"Does this have anything to do with the interesting design you have shaved on your pussy?"

"Pussy yes, but the wrong pussy…"

Björk chooses that moment to prance past us, a buzzed stripe across her back, and meows loudly as if to tattle on me.

"Oops," I mutter and chance a nervous look at him. "It was an accident. A little slip of the wrist."

"An accident," he mirrors. He runs his finger along his cat's bald spot and chuckles. Then he looks between us and points at my naked sex. "So how did you 'accidentally' shave an M onto your pussy, hmm? A little flick of the wrist?"

I scoff and look down at my beautiful W.

My very upside down W.

"Oops."

Will is gone early this fine Monday morning. A big meeting and all that jazz. It gave me time to lounge around the house and officially apologize to Björk for Saturday. I even played her favorite song, "Big Time Sensuality," by the real Björk. Oddly enough, after the razor mishap, she's more respectful of her elders. She knows who's boss now. And if she gets a little too close for comfort, I just have to say, "Bzzzzz," before she's darting for cover under the nearest piece of furniture.

I'm all smiles as I grab my stuff and head out to my car to go to work. Big D would love me if I brought some Mickey Ds into the office today. I feel like a super adult this morning all on time and thinking of others. Thunder grumbles in the distance, but I won't let it rain on my sunny morning.

All happiness bleeds out of me when I see my father leaned up against his car, a scowl marring his features. This isn't the "I'm disappointed in you, Lilith" scowl either. It's the one he reserves for his opponents across the business table.

This means war.

Lifting my chin, I face him head-on. I'm unafraid of what he'll throw at me. Will and I are strong. Unbreakable. And no matter what he tries to do to break us up, it won't work.

That is...until he opens his mouth.

His words come tumbling from his lips, and I realize my dad is king for a reason.

And I'm nothing more than a princess he intends on locking in a tower.

My happily ever after is officially over.

Chapter Nineteen

Will

Mondays are for Making Lance
Eat a Knuckle Sandwich

Restructuring.

That was my warning from my boss at this morning's meeting. But it smelled fishy. Super fishy. Like Bart Hamilton trying to meddle in my life because he's a damn prick kind of fishy. My boss stated that shit was about to hit the fan and that it would benefit me to start looking for a new job and soon.

I'm the best damn internal auditor they have.

I can't believe I even tried to help her father. Won't make that mistake again. I pull out my phone once I'm inside my office and text Lilith.

Me: I think I might be getting fired soon.

She doesn't respond and I get caught up on working on my résumé until lunch. I check my watch and then my phone. Still no response.

Me: Call me when you get a chance, babe.

Another half hour goes by.

I call and she doesn't answer. I call again and again.

Me: Please answer. I'm worried.

Crickets.

I turn on my computer and switch on her radio show. It doesn't take long for me to realize she's not on the air today. Big D is solo and doesn't allude to where she's at. Maybe she's sick.

Unease trickles through me. I won't feel good until I speak to her. Since I'm probably getting let go soon anyway, I shut down my office for the day and go hunting for my girlfriend. Her radio station is closest, so I swing by there first. But when I realize her car isn't in the lot, I keep on my way home, calling her along the way.

No answer.

What the fuck?

By the time I reach our neighborhood, my anxiety is at an all-time high. Lilith is a grown woman and has things she does, but it's unlike her not to talk to me all day. I'm freaking the fuck out that she's hurt or something.

When I make it to our street, I'm thankful to see a car in her driveway. I think it's her car at first until I realize it's just another red, shiny vehicle but doesn't belong to her. A man in a suit is taking pictures of her house. I pull into my driveway and barely get the key out of the ignition before I'm stalking over to him.

"Can I help you?" I growl as I approach.

The man turns, flashing me a megawatt smile. "Killian Vanderpool at your service. They call me the realtor with the *kille*r deals." He winks at me. "Would you like to take a peek inside? This one's new on the market today."

"This is my girlfriend's house. She's not selling it," I snap, irritation making my blood begin to boil.

His brows furrow together. "I've been on the phone with the homeowner all morning working to get this house on the market. I'm sorry, but if you'll excuse me, sir, I have to get this property on my website today." He trades his camera for a sign that he pulls from the trunk.

For Sale.

Killian Vanderpool's big smile is splashed across the sign and I want to punch a hole through it.

With gritted teeth, I dial Lilith again. No answer. I'm a storm about to let loose if I don't get in touch with my girl-friend. This is unlike her.

I call the station and land in a queue as I climb into my car. Big D is babbling about a Meg Myers concert coming to town on the radio.

"Caller number nine, you've won tickets to—"

"Where's Lil?" I demand, cutting off Big D.

"The infamous Wonka," he says with a chuckle. "My partner in crime is taking a day of vacation."

"I need to know." My voice is low and deadly.

"Ahhh, a Tom Petty & The Heartbreakers fan. I've got ya, dawg."

"I Need to Know" starts playing on the speakers and I almost hang up when he comes through the line again.

"She quit this morning, Wonka," he hisses, as if he's trying to be quiet. "She called me in fuckin' tears and quit. Before I could ask her what's up, she hung up. Somethin' didn't sound right with my girl. I thought maybe it had somethin' to do with you, man."

I blink in confusion as I haul ass out of the neighbor-hood. "It's not me, I can assure you. She put her house up on the market too. Something is wrong and I'm going to find out. She loves that job, so there's no way she'd just up and quit."

"Back at ya, brother. Her ghostin' you like this is fucked up. I'm wonderin' if it has somethin' to do with Daddy

Warbucks. He's always on her shit."

A growl rumbles from me. "Did you tell anyone about her quitting?"

"No, man. I was hoping she was just having her period or was hungover. I didn't tell Leon. He thinks she's got the shits and is contagious. Find our girl and tell her to get her skinny ass back to work."

"Thanks, D."

I hang up and haul ass toward Hamilton Investments.

The entire time I drive, I try her cell. Restructuring at my job. Her quitting hers. The for-sale sign in her yard. Her ghosting me. This all reeks of Bart Hamilton. Fucking bastard.

I'm tired of this asshole bullying my girl.

Hang on, Lilith, I'm going to make this right.

I storm past the receptionist, uncaring of the way her heels clack after me. She calls out to me, but I ignore her, opting to pay Bart a surprise visit. When I burst through his door, the smug fuck leans back in his leather chair and flashes me a wide grin.

This isn't the smile of a man whose daughter's life he's single-handedly ruining.

No, this is the smile of a man who thinks he's just won a game. A deal. Some match that wasn't particularly even to begin with. Why the hell he's so dead set on hating me, I'll never know. But screwing with Lilith's life like this is unforgiveable. It makes him the shittiest parent in my book.

"Mr. Grant. Fancy seeing you here," he greets, smirking.

I charge over to his desk and slam my palms down on the solid surface. My glare must be scary as fuck because his eyes widen for a moment as he rolls back in his chair.

"I've called security," the receptionist says from the doorway.

He raises a palm. "We're two grown men who are going to talk like adults. Just have them wait outside, Tiffany, in case Mr. Grant decides to start acting like a child."

She closes the door with a soft click and I growl at him.

"Where the fuck is my girlfriend?"

His nostrils flare and he rises from his chair, no doubt hating the disadvantage of being seated. He straightens his jacket as he sneers at me. "My daughter is done with her sabbatical. The little rebellious vacation of hers is over."

I stand up straight and crack my neck, rolling it over my shoulders. My hands form into fists. It takes everything in me not to pummel this motherfucker. "Whatever bullshit you've filled her head with to get her to agree to this is just that…bullshit. Tell me where she is. I need to talk to her."

"So you can bully her into staying, Mr. Grant?" He huffs and his face burns bright red with anger. "Your past is a nasty stain that will soil the pure future of my daughter. Lilith has had her fun, but it's time for her to get serious. There are things—people—who have been waiting on her for a long time. As her father, it's my duty to be firm with her when she's making the wrong decisions."

I clench my jaw and shake my head. "Lilith isn't some business deal," I snap. "She's my girlfriend and she deserves better than this. Do you even hear yourself right now? You'll make her hate you."

"Says the man with no father himself. How is Barbara anyhow? Your grandma still living in the duplex on Oak

Avenue? I happen to know the fella who owns those duplexes over there. He mentioned he might be interested in selling. What a shame to have poor granny out on her fanny."

Realization washes over me in a wave.

He's threatened beyond taking away my girlfriend's house.

Bart Hamilton, that dirty dog, used me and my fucking grandma to get Lilith to do his bidding.

I'm pissed as fuck at this man but mostly, I feel pity for him. He's so caught up in having his perfect world and perfect family that he doesn't realize it's blowing up in his face.

"It'll catch up to you," I tell him, my voice cold and calm. "You're so busy putting up this façade that you're destroying the very foundation of everything you fucking care about. Your company. Your daughter. Sure, you may have won thinking you'll intimidate her into going home, but you've done nothing but break her heart. A dad is supposed to love and guide his daughter. And one day, I'll show *your grandchildren* how a real damn daddy is supposed to act. Now tell me where Lilith is before I throw your goddamned desk out that window." I point to the glass and glower at him with every ounce of hate and hostility I have in me.

He blinks in shock, momentarily stunned by my words, but then sneers. "As soon as we arrived earlier, she told me she was going to go see Lance. You remember him? The successful, wealthy, worthy Lance Peterson."

I don't spare him another glance as I stalk out of his office.

"*Lance* is going to make her very happy," he calls out, his robust voice chuckling behind me.

And *I'm* going to make Lance eat a knuckle sandwich.

Right before I steal the girl who makes me very happy.

Lance's office isn't far from Bart's and I'm unnerved when I see Lilith's cherry red Mustang parked crookedly in front of a meter outside a tall building. Her meter is almost up, so I shove some change into it so she won't get a ticket before I hurry inside. The building is fancy as fuck, reminding me I'm just a damn boring bank auditor.

But boring bank auditor or not, *I* know how to make Lilith smile.

I know how to make her laugh.

I know how to make her come.

Lance, the successful lawyer, doesn't know her like I do. He doesn't know she likes fifteen extra minutes to sleep in. That you have to set the alarm fifteen minutes early to trick her so she won't be late. He doesn't know she secretly loves cinnamon even though she claims it's not her fave. Because when I make her coffee and add a pinch, she always gushes about how much better coffee is those mornings. Lance, the motherfucking boring billionaire in training, doesn't know Lilith loves hip-hop rap from the nineties and can sing every single word in annoying perfection. The asshole doesn't know she cries every damn time during the SPCA commercials and snort laughs at every episode of *Friends*. He doesn't know she'll claim her clit is too sensitive to be touched anymore but will grind it against the heel of your palm, greedy for just one more orgasm. And what he really doesn't know about her is her eyes shimmer with delight when you brush the hair from her face, kiss her nose, and tell her she's the most beautiful girl in the world.

Lance doesn't know shit about her.

Because she's not his.

She's mine, dammit.

I'm met with more gatekeepers at this building, but I ignore them all as I locate his suite number on a board near the elevators. More clacking of heels run after me as I stalk down the idiot who thinks he can take my girl.

Even his office is ritzy and pretentious. A silver, shiny plate indicating his name on his door. Big, expensive mahogany separating me from her. I turn the knob and push through. As soon as I see her, I let out a sigh of relief.

That is, until I take in the scene.

Lance, the balding motherfucker, grins at her as she laughs—fucking laughs—at whatever he's just said. Chinese food is spread out all over his desk. Food they've apparently just eaten together. She's beautiful today but doesn't look like herself. No, she's gone full-on *Hamilton from the Hamptons* in her white cardigan, smooth brown hair pulled into a neat ponytail, and a knee-length pale yellow dress.

When he sees me, he straightens and his smile falls.

Yeah, you better stop looking at my woman like that, motherfucker.

"Mr. Grant," he says smoothly.

Lilith snaps her head my way and gapes in surprise. Her eyes are swollen from crying at some point in the day, but her makeup has been touched up. A lingering smile remains on her lips.

What sort of alternate reality have I walked into?

"Lilith," I bark, my blood boiling with fury at her father and confusion at the way she's dressed. "Why are you here?"

Lance rises. "Mr. Grant, if you'd like to make an appointment, my secretary—"

"Does it look like I want a goddamned appointment with you?" I roar, my rage rattling its cage inside me. "I came for her." I point at my girl.

Tears well in her eyes and she shakes her head. "You have to leave, Will."

I deflate like a balloon. "What?"

When I take a step toward her, Lance comes around the desk and intercepts me. "You heard the lady," he starts.

"I suggest you move or I'll make you move," I threaten.

Lilith jumps to her feet and grips his arm. My eyes dart down to how she clutches him. Acid bubbles in my veins. I don't understand what's happening here.

"You can't be here," she chokes out, tears rolling down her cheeks.

"The hell I can't," I snap. "You can't do this to me, Lil. I was so fucking scared out of my mind. I want to know what the hell is going on with you right now."

"As her attorney—"

Lance's words die in his throat when I snap my fiery gaze his way.

"Her attorney?" I seethe.

She releases him and steps my way. Confusion may be clouding around us, but my body seeks hers. I eat up the distance and haul her into my arms. At first, she's stiff, but then she relaxes in my grip. Her fingers grip at my dress shirt as she whispers tearfully. "Will, listen to me, you have to leave."

Gripping her biceps, I pull her away from me. Her watery eyes plead with me to understand. I don't fucking understand.

"No," I snap, my eyes falling to her trembling bottom lip. "I'm not going anywhere without you, baby. Don't make me carry you out of here over my shoulder because I so fucking will."

She laughs through a sob. "You're so stubborn."

I slide my palms to her cheeks and kiss her red nose. "You're mine," I murmur as if that explains everything.

She sniffles. "I'm trying to fix things. Why can't you just let me fix it?"

"Nothing is broken. We're perfect," I tell her, my voice hoarse.

"But he was going to break everything. I was just trying to fix it for us."

I jerk my head to glower at Lance. He holds his hands up in defense and says, "Not me."

"Daddy," she utters, dragging my gaze back to hers. "He…"

"Was going to get me fired?"

Tears roll down her cheeks as she nods. "And Babs…"

"Grandma can handle herself," I assure her. "As for me, my job means nothing if I don't have you to come home to. Why didn't you tell me your dad was up to more shit?"

"His threats were so awful. He said he could ruin you in an instant. Your career. Your grandma's home. Your reputation. To make it all go away, all I had to do was go home and meet with Lance." She smiles. "So I did exactly as Daddy asked. I'm here. Meeting with Lance."

"And as her attorney," he says, visibly wincing at my hateful stare. "I've been advising her on what to do." He chuckles nervously. "Not whatever is going through that head of yours, Mr. Grant. I've known that ship between us sailed a long time ago. Her parents and mine have had these grandiose ideas of us dating, but I didn't have the heart to tell them I've been seeing my massage therapist for months."

"She's pregnant," Lilith tells me happily. "And using my

advice, he's going to tell his parents to shove it and marry Gillian."

Lilith's lips beg to be kissed, so I press my mouth to hers. Then I lean my forehead against hers. "And what's your attorney's advice?" I question, grateful to have her in my arms.

"To talk to you," she murmurs, her hot breath tickling my face as her lips hover close to mine.

"Smart man," I say. "And what did he suggest we talk about?"

"He wanted me to ask you if I was worth it. Was I, Lilith Hamilton, worth all the hell my father was going to rain down on your life." She sighs. "I mean, he has the power to make me homeless and jobless, your grandma homeless, and you jobless. Am I worth all that stress?"

My palms slide to her bottom through her prissy dress and I squeeze, uncaring that Lance is a witness to our intimate reunion. "Of course you're fucking worth it, baby. I'd live down by the river with you, Grandma, Skippy, and Björk in a cardboard box if that meant I got to wake up to your sweet smile each morning."

"Oh, he's good," Lance chimes in from nearby. "I'm using that line on Gillian."

I smirk and then kiss her pretty mouth. "So what are you going to tell your mean, meddling daddy?"

"I'm going to tell him to go fuck himself."

Chapter Twenty

Lilith

Wednesdays are for Breaking Ratings

Three weeks later...

"**A**nd there you have it, folks. 'The End' by The Doors. Kinda symbolic right now for—"

"For how when one door closes, one opens. That's right, Lil. Let's take a break before our morning commute updates and coffee call-ins. We'll have a special guest on today too so make sure to tune in." The *Live on Air* light goes off, and D pulls his headphones from his ears. "Girl, you need to quit it with this funk. I thought things were good on the home front. You've been like this ever since you came back from your hiatus."

"It wasn't a hiatus. I really quit."

Daryl laughs and rolls his eyes at me. "Yeah, and that's why your man carried you back in here the next day and sat you on your chair, kissed you, and told you to have a nice day?"

Okay, fine, hiatus, but in the moment of panic, I did quit. I let the fear of my father's reach control me yet again. He threatened to ruin Will, and I believed him. I knew he could and I damn well knew he would. I had finally caved to the realization that my father had finally won. He held all the cards, and as I folded and went home, there was one last hand I never expected.

Lance.

When Daddy handed me over to him as if I were nothing more than a contestant prize, what happened next practically sideswiped me. Lance thanked my father, shut his door, and as he kindly asked me to sit and I not so kindly told him to do a lot of awful things, he went on, while we both stood there, and talked, shocking the shit out of me.

Lance, in fact, was not there to claim his prize and walk me down the aisle. Little had I known, he was actually in love with someone else, and they were having a baby. It took him until now to realize how awful my father was to me, and he had no intentions of being any part of ruining my happiness. In fact, he wanted to help guarantee it.

And so the planning began.

Turns out, Daddy Dearest didn't have as much control as he thought. Since Lance had been so close with my father, he had learned a few things along the way. One being that my mother, bless her heart, had set up a trust fund for me when I moved out. It was never mentioned to me because, per my mother, I wanted nothing to do with money, but she did tell Lance. She must be a little like me behind her plastic façade because she set up the fund, just in case, knowing my father and I would probably come to blows over everything eventually.

So despite my father no doubt planning to cut me off if I don't play by his rules, I have quite the nest egg in my trust fund thanks to Mom.

One of my biggest concerns was my house. Despite Daddy pulling in a realtor and trying to sell my house right out from under me, it was illegal to do so. He was bluffing and hoping I wouldn't call him on it. The deed, though, is in my name. Even if it was his money that paid for the damn thing. My attorney, good ol' comb-over Lance, assured me Daddy didn't have a bucket to piss in.

Lance also said he would do what he could about Will's job. He thought maybe he'd have some sway with Daddy and remind him that what he's doing is harassment. However, he didn't know how much power he had regarding the sale of Babs's duplex. The worst part of the conversation was the station. My father was throwing a lot of money to purchase it. More than it was worth. And there was no way they wouldn't take the deal. I offered to buy the station myself, but too many hoops had to be jumped through to make that happen. And Lance guaranteed I wouldn't make it through the first hoop before my father caught wind and shut me down.

Lance was trying to cheer me up, telling me I could always start a podcast out of my house when Will busted through that door ready to avenge and rescue me. It was the most romantic thing I've ever witnessed. After Lance and I explained, Will shook his hand and carried me out of there.

Once we made it back to Will's, he made me vow that no matter what or who tries to come between us, it will never be strong enough to tear us apart or break us. He vowed so, after taking me in absolutely every single position in his house. Kamasutra would be jealous.

Everything was perfect. I was no longer in the clutches of my father and Will and I were finally at peace and happy. The only thing lingering was the sale of the station. I expected my father to pull the plug within hours of me reconciling with Will. But when I came back to work the next day and sat there, as any other day waiting for the lights to go off, they never did.

I know my father. He doesn't make a promise he doesn't keep. So the past three weeks have been a torturous waiting game for me. I know this horrible secret and I am not sure what to do with it. Daryl is gonna lose his job, along with a lot of other hard-working employees. How am I supposed to break it to my best friend that he's no longer going to be able to feed his taco addiction? And so every day, I come to work with the anticipation that today will be the day.

"I'm your best friend, girl. Don't do that disappearing shit to me again," Daryl says, interrupting me from my thoughts.

"Whatever. I wanted to see if I went missing if you would send a secret agent to come searching for me. Show how much I mean to you." I laugh. "Speaking of secret, you ever gonna tell me who the secret guest is today? I've guessed every single one of my favorite bands, so I need to know if I should start thinking other genres or possibly actors. I do have a fancy for Gerald Butler, ya know."

Daryl grabs a cookie from the plate I brought in and shoves it in his mouth. "Can't ruin the surprise. Plus, I really think this might help with ratings."

Doubtful.

Ever since word got out about an investor searching out the station, it's been hard to schedule bands. Agents worry that if the station sells, it won't stick to the same music genre, which could be bad for their clients. A lot of times in this case, it changes. They question the success and if it's worth their clients' time to travel just to do a radio show. *Politics.* Leon moans anytime he gets the report each day.

Will also stopped calling into the station. My request. I

loved his dedication. Our callers loved his dedication. But I wanted us to be us. I didn't want to rehash my life every day on the station. It was like living in a "scenes from last week's episode" part of television shows. Trust me, I already knew what happened. I was there.

Callers moaned and groaned about it. Polls and emails were sent to get Wonka back on the air. But I had to believe our station would thrive because we were two awesome DJs and not because of my neighbor.

"Well, then I'm going with Steven Tyler. If anyone can save the station's ratings, it's definitely the lead singer of Aerosmith."

The commercial ends and Daryl goes into the morning commute stats. This being the time when Will normally calls, it does bring a sadness to me. I won't lie and say I do kinda miss hearing his voice each day on the radio.

"All right, listeners, I know I've been keeping you all on your toes about our secret guest today, and it's time for the reveal. Lil, wanna take a last guess on who you think it could be?"

"Well, D, I gotta say I'm out of ideas. Bring us our guest."

"Nah, I say you phone a friend before you give up."

I look at him, wondering where he's going with this. "I Immm. Not sure who I would call."

"Let me help you out. Hello, caller, you're on the air."

"Hey there, Big D."

My heart skips at the sound of Will's voice. I give Daryl the questioning eye. What's he up to?

"Sup, Wonka! Long time no talk. Man, our callers missed you."

"Thanks, Big D. I missed calling in. I have so much to

say and tell everyone."

"Wonka," I warn. "Don't you think you should just keep your dirty little secrets to yourself from now on? What would your neighbor think if she knew you were exploiting all your special moments on air with a million listeners?"

"I think she would enjoy getting to hear me talk about how much I love her. How my life hasn't been the same since she recklessly stormed into it. I think the listeners would love to hear how since finding the love of my life, I haven't thought of anything else but making her mine."

The door to the station opens and Will walks in, his phone still to his ear.

"Wh-what are you doing here?" I throw my hand over my mic, gaping at him.

"Listeners, I'd like to welcome Mr. Wonka, our secret guest to the station," Daryl says.

I snap my attention to Daryl. "What? What's going on?"

Will hangs up his phone and walks over to me. My eyes go wide. Confusion is prominent on my face. Will stops in front of my chair and bends down, pulling the mic to him.

"You see, listeners, I feel like, since you've been with me from the beginning, it's important I fill you in on one last plan I have up my sleeve before I officially sign off."

"Will—I mean Wonka, what are you doing here?" I ask, trying, *not sure why*, to still conceal his identity.

"I'm telling the world that I am in love with a girl who brings so much color into my life. And I'm not referring to my pink coffee maker, or the red thongs hanging from my bedpost."

I throw my hand over his mouth to shut him up.

He laughs and dodges me, bringing the mic back to his lips. "Big D, do you think it's okay if I steal the show for just a moment?"

Daryl is smiling so wide you'd think he won the endless tacos at Manny's lottery. "Have at it, Wonka!" He chuckles into his mic.

I turn to Will. I'm about to roll my eyes at him and his theatrics when he kneels before me.

"What are you doing?" I whisper softly, my nerves going haywire.

"I'm telling the entire world how much I love my neighbor." Will reaches into his back pocket and pulls out a small black box. "Lilith Hamilton, my feisty, beautiful, one-of-a-kind, crazy neighbor. I haven't had a good night's sleep since the day you fell into my life."

I go to smack him, but he dodges me once again.

"Since night one, I've lain in my bed long after you've fallen asleep in my arms and thought how my life will never be the same. You have changed me. You've made me whole and happy. My heart belongs to you. We may have started as just neighbors, but I want us to end with you being my wife."

Will opens the box to a simple princess cut diamond shining back at me. Everything around me has gone silent. I gaze at the beautiful ring and lift my teary eyes to him.

"Will…"

"Or Wonka, if you prefer."

I laugh through my overflow of tears. I look back at the ring in shock. Oh my God, he just proposed to me!

"Your silence is killing us listeners, Lil," Daryl chimes in.

Shit, right. I lift my hands to cup Will's face. "You've been and will always be my hero. My savior. You saved me. You forever have my heart. My love…" I have to stop to wipe the tears off my face so I can see. "Are you sure you want someone who's probably gonna break things, leave dishes around, walk over the grass when it's freshly cut, and possibly never do her own laundry?"

Will smiles, leaving me breathless. His hands go up and now it's him cupping my cheeks. "I'd even let you break my coffee machine and shave my pussy again, as long as it meant you'd always be mine."

Daryl gasps, and I laugh. "You two better explain that one."

"Lil, baby. What's it going to be? Will you make me the happiest man alive or am I going to have to kidnap you?"

I stall just a second to mess with him, but then I stick my hand out. "Yes. God, yes. I'll marry you." I throw my arms around him and our lips connect in what feels like the most intense kiss yet.

"I love you, Lilith Hamilton," he whispers against my mouth, then pulls away, sliding the ring on my finger.

"And there you have it, folks. A shocking reveal *and* a proposal. Congrats Will and Lil! Or should I say Mr. Wonka and his naughty neighbor?"

I thought Leon was never going to let us leave. I also thought Leon was going to steal my ring. I get the whole bromance thing, but God, offering Will a spot on our radio show was going a little too far.

"I'm not sure why you turned the idea down. I would make a great radio host. Your listeners love me."

I smack at Will's chest as we walk out of the station. "Yeah, well, I don't want to be out of a job because it went from the Lil and Big D show to the Wonka and Big D show.

I swear he was about three seconds away from replacing me with you."

"Don't worry, baby," Will says playfully. "I much prefer our private Lil and Will show." He chuckles and throws his arm around me. We walk out the front doors of the station and turn toward my car when I stop in my tracks.

My body tenses immediately at the sight of my father leaned against his car parked beside mine. "What are you doing here?" I ask him.

He frowns at my curt tone. "I want to talk to you."

"Talk to my attorney," I spit back.

"Nonsense. I don't need Lance to talk to my own daughter." His voice rises.

Will takes a step toward him, but I pull him back. "Will, don't. He's not worth it. Let's just go." I turn my back to my father and we start to walk away.

"I'm sorry for what I've done."

His words stop me in my tracks. Specific words I've never heard come from Bart Hamilton's mouth. I turn around. "You're *sorry*? For what? Trying to control me? For attempting to ruin and take away everything I love?"

"I'm sorry for it all," he states.

I stare at him in confusion. The man before me is not my father.

"Please," he begs. "I would like five minutes of your time."

I turn to Will for guidance.

"I don't want him upsetting you," he growls.

"That is the last thing I want," my father chimes in.

Will offers him a glare, but softens when he brings his eyes back to me. "If he says anything to hurt you, walk away. I'm right over here if you need me." He kisses me on the forehead and walks to his car. I wait until I watch him shut his door and turn back to my father.

"You have three minutes."

He nods, takes a slow step toward me, and stops. "I listened to you, you know. Ever since you started at this place. Every morning."

The news shocks me. "Why?"

"Because you're my daughter. Because I want to know about you. I want to know how your life is."

"Okay, great, you could have just called and asked. Or was that when you called and demanded things from me?"

I know that comment hurts him.

"I shouldn't have tried to control you."

"No, you shouldn't've," I agree, raising my voice. "You want to know about me? You could have asked."

"I didn't know how," he admits. "I know I've done you wrong. I've made many mistakes when it's come to you. But one thing I never want you to question is my love for you."

"Don't try and feed me lies. Nothing you have done shows love for a daughter."

He takes another slow step toward me. "You're right. I've been awful. I've been controlling. I've been wrong."

His words. They're words I've been waiting all my life to hear. "Why now?"

"It may be hard for you to believe after how awful I've been, but I've only ever wanted you to be this amazing person." He frowns. "But in my vision, I only saw what I wanted. I never considered what you wanted. I let my power and need to control the situation get in the way of that. I guess I was too blinded by what I wanted to realize." He stalls for a quick second. "And possibly a good ol' hair raising lecture from your mother. She may be set in her own ways, but she

loves you just as much. It took her reminding me how much greater the loss would be if I didn't make it right with you. I don't want you to hate me. But I understand if you do. I just came here to tell you I'm sorry. I've pulled back on all accounts. You won't have any problems with the house. I couldn't really sell it because it didn't belong to me. I was just bluffing so you'd come home. I'm sorry, Lilith."

I'm blown away at his confession. Never have I seen this side of my father. I look at him and I see sadness. Truth. Remorse.

"And the station? Will?"

"The station has been bought," he says.

My anger shoots right back up. "See, you—"

"I bought it to give it to you. It's yours. I'll sign the deed over to you and WXOJ will be yours to do what you will. You're amazing at what you do and with your talent and ideas, I know you can make that place shine."

My mouth hangs open. "You bought me the station?"

Daddy always tries to buy himself out of trouble. This time, it might actually work because I do love that place.

"I hope you don't mind. The place was hurting financially, and if it wasn't me, it would have been someone else. They were searching to sell, so unless I made the move, they would have sold eventually. I heard a new country station was in talks of buying this place." Daddy blanches after saying that and I can't help but laugh. My father just made a joke.

"I love you, Lilith. I am truly sorry for my actions. I just want you in my life."

My eyes shed tears for a second time. I stare at my father until I find myself running and throwing myself in his arms. "Thank you," I whisper, hugging him.

He wraps his large arms around me and hugs me back. His lips press against the top of my head.

"No, thank you for being my amazing daughter."

I pull away, wiping the tears off my cheeks. "Maybe you can come over to the house and continue telling me how amazing this daughter of yours is over a Manhattan and some barbeque. And then I can brag about how my *fiancé* makes a mean steak."

"Speaking of William," he says, his features growing stormy.

I wince, waiting for the hate to spew.

"He was right."

Blinking at him, I mutter, "Come again?"

"He was right about everything. You. Me." He growls. "Charles Britton."

"Who's Charles Britton?" My brows furrow together in confusion.

He frowns. "He was the CFO of Hamilton Investments."

"Was?"

"William saw it. He saw it from a million miles away. It was right in front of me and I was too blind to see. Too blind worrying about getting you back home. Charles was embezzling from the firm, Lilith. Your fiancé told me so." He lets out a frustrated breath. "I thought he was just riling me up, but then I actually took a look at the documents he gave me and then did a little investigating on my own. I need to apologize to him because he tried to help. Even when I was being a total monster, Mr. Grant was looking out for our family."

My eyes are wide with shock. Will never spoke of it to me. I'm going to tie him up later and spank him with his own belt for keeping this from me. Until then, though...

"You tried to get him fired."

Thank God Will was able to hold onto his job. After Daddy realized I hired Lance rather than jumped into marriage with him, he backed off of everything. The "restructuring" at Will's company never happened and he's still the bank nerd he always was.

"I did," he agrees. "It was wrong. Which is why…" He flashes me one of his winning smiles that has sealed him all kinds of deals in his career. "I'm going to offer him a job."

I hug my father and for once a wall of resentment doesn't stand between us. He squeezes me back.

"But first, steak," he says, patting my back.

Pulling away, I grin at him. "The *best* steak."

Epilogue
Will

Fridays are not for Anal

Five years later…

I stare across the boardroom table at Hamilton Investments and pin him with my no-nonsense glare. I've gone over the facts, obsessed over the details, and come to a conclusion.

He's guilty.

No way around it.

"Numbers don't lie," I tell him, my glare unwavering.

Liam narrows his stare at me, unfazed by my scrutiny. "I didn't steal it."

Bart, who's sitting to my left, raises his brows in shock. My father-in-law knows it. We *both* know it. Liam did this and he's going to confess. And once he confesses, we'll proceed from there.

"You were the only one who had access to the funds during that time period," I tell him, my voice calm despite my irritation.

"Maybe you just miscounted," Bart offers, always a sucker when it comes to these conversations. He may be the owner of Hamilton Investments and me just his internal auditor now, but I'm running this show.

"I didn't miscount. We all know I never miscount," I reply, my sharp stare never leaving the young man sitting to my right.

Liam shifts in his seat and scribbles something down on the paper in front of him. I ignore his loss of focus as I wait for my confession.

"It's late," Bart mutters under his breath. "We have dinner reservations later. Tonya's probably already there waiting. Maybe we should just let this go."

I swivel in my chair and lift a brow at him. "Charles Britton stole from you and he is sitting in prison as we speak. At Hamilton Investments, we don't tolerate stealing," I growl, reminding the old man that he needs to stay focused. He's too soft in his old age.

Bart groans but concedes with a nod. I turn back to Liam. His brown eyes meet mine and he grins at me. Challenging and fearless. It knocks me off my guard. It always does. Apparently, I'm weak in my old age too.

"I didn't steal it," he says again, but the smirk on his face determines otherwise.

I'm starting to believe that maybe I didn't count right. But that's madness. I am never wrong. At least about numbers I'm not.

Bart checks his watch as I'm about to start another grueling round of questions. We're interrupted when Lilith waltzes in the room, a picture of sunshine.

And by waltzes, I mean waddles.

My beautiful wife is pregnant and the little girl in her tummy is due any time.

All irritation over the thief sitting beside me dissolves as I rise to meet her. Liam is quicker. He slides out of the chair, snags his paper, straightens his red bowtie that matches mine exactly, and then saunters over to my woman.

"I got you a present, Mommy." He beams, holding out the paper of what I think might be a hand drawn picture of Björk. It's messy, but he's a kid, so…

"Aww," she coos as she admires his picture. "It's beautiful. Björk is the prettiest kitty I ever did see."

The little shit then reaches into his back pocket and pulls out a bag of Skittles. Skittles I know he purchased using the dollar he stole out of my office drawer.

Bart laughs and I shake my head. I'll have to ground my four-year-old son later for stealing and lying, but for now, I let him be a gentleman for his mother. She runs her fingers through his hair that's the same shade as mine and flashes him a brilliant smile.

"Thank you, baby. I love Skittles. But you know who loves them more?" she asks.

"My sister?"

"Yes!" She claps her hands and then pulls him to her for a hug.

"You guys ready?" Bart questions as he holds his hand out.

Liam breaks away from his mom and grabs onto his grandpa's hand. I overhear Bart explaining to his grandson that stealing is for weak men and Hamilton men aren't weak. I can't help but smirk when William Grant, Junior reminds his grandpa that he's not a Hamilton.

"Let me guess," Lilith says, amusement in her voice. "He didn't earn the money to buy me those Skittles from the vending machine?"

I turn and admire my gorgeous wife. Pregnancy looks good on her. She's fearless and bright in a sunny yellow dress that showcases her very pregnant belly. The matte red on her lips is sexy as fuck and the moment Liam leaves after dinner to spend the night with his grandparents, I'm going to spend the rest of the night sucking it off.

"Not even close but come tomorrow evening when he gets back from your parents', he's going to be pulling weeds in the flowerbed. That'll teach him," I say with a grunt.

She laughs and the sound fills my soul. "You think he's going to feel punished by doing yardwork? He's just like you, Wonka. Exactly like you down to the freaking bowtie. You're not punishing him. The little turkey is going to enjoy every second of it."

I grab her hands and pull her to me, loving the way her giant belly presses against me. Our mouths meet and I kiss her pretty mouth.

"He can't go unpunished," I murmur against her lips.

"Maybe I could take his punishment for him. He gave *me* the Skittles after all," she teases.

My palms slide to her ass through her dress and I give her fleshy bottom a playful slap. "There. Punishment successfully transferred."

She laughs as she grips my bowtie and pulls me forward. "I think you might have to do that a few more times later tonight. Our son wasn't the only one who was bad today."

I slide my palm into her silky hair and tug her hair until she's looking up at me. "What did you do?" My brow is lifted in question.

Her brown eyes twinkle with a challenge—the same look our son gives me when he's up to something. "You'll have to see later…"

"Did you try to paint our kitchen pink again?"

"Nope."

"Does my cat have all her hair?"

"Björk is still the beautiful crazy pussy she always is."

"Did you throw out my lactose-free coffee creamer?"

"As much as I hate that shit, no."

"Is my new azalea bush still alive?"

She snorts. "Yep."

"What could you have possibly done to get yourself in trouble?"

"I found a renter for the house." Her eyes twinkle with mischief.

I frown in confusion. "The lease was up and the Carlsons were moving to the city. It was in the plan to rent it out." For years now, we've rented her old home out ever since she moved in with me. We tried to convince my grandma to move in next door, but she really does love her duplex and said Lil's old house is too big for her and Skippy.

"Yeah, but…"

"But what?"

"I rented it out to Daryl and his sweet girlfriend."

I blink in shock. Horror rushes through me. "You didn't."

"Majick isn't that bad once you get to know her—"

"You didn't."

"—she only has seven dogs and—"

"You didn't."

"—that one time she accidentally flooded the radio station wasn't her fault—"

"You didn't."

"—not to mention Big D loves her—"

"You didn't."

"—and the time she hid in your trunk because the police were after her for indecent exposure was all a misunderstanding—"

"You didn't."

"—plus, she's practically family since D knocked her up—"

"Lilith," I growl. "Tell me we are not about to be neighbors with Majick. I can handle Daryl, but that woman… she's insane."

She lifts a brow. "You thought *I* was insane once too."

"The jury is still out on that one," I deadpan.

"Brat," she says with a huff, a smile tilting her lips on one side.

"You're definitely getting punished for this one." I groan. Majick is worse than insane. She's fucking psychotic. "Majick. Fuck."

She laughs. "I don't really see what could go wrong. She's a sweetheart."

"She's never babysitting."

"You drive a hard bargain," she says, giggling.

Just imagining Majick with her wild blond hair with pink streaks, four lip piercings, and seven dogs terrorizing our rental property next door has my eye twitching. The thought of her ever being responsible for my little Liam has my head throbbing.

Never. Never babysitting. Hell, I don't even want her near my lawn, much less my kids.

"Hey, Wonka?" my wife asks, her voice filled with amusement, drawing me from my daze.

"What, woman?"

"I'm just fuckin' with ya."

My breath rushes out loudly in relief. "You're right," I growl. "You're definitely getting punished for this. Your antics are too crazy."

She grins, showing all her pearly white teeth. "Darn. My big handsome husband is going to tie me up and spank my ass," she sasses as she pulls away and starts for the door. "Oh, the horror."

I stalk after her and give her juicy ass a little swat. "Spanking isn't the only thing I'm going to do with that ass."

"Will!" she exclaims in faux horror. My wife may act scandalized, but she loves me in every one of her tight little holes. "Fridays are *not* for anal."

Flashing her a wolfish grin, I shrug. "We'll see, demon girl."

"Careful there, Wonka, you might just wake up to a neighbor from hell," she warns. "Majick and D really are house hunting."

"Wouldn't be the first time I had a neighbor from hell."

"And look how that turned out for you." She motions at her voluptuous pregnant body. "You got an angel."

At this, I laugh. "You're the filthiest angel I've ever met."

"To my defense, you made me filthy. I was pretty angel- ic before you. You definitely made me that way."

"*You* made *me* this way," I say back, motioning at myself.

"And what way is that?" she challenges.

I palm her stomach and smile. "Happy."

Fridays may not be for anal.

But Fridays *are* for quickie boardroom sex with your pregnant wife.

Saturdays are for pulling weeds and lessons learned for little lie tellers.

And Sundays?

Sundays are for hangovers when you're drunk on love.

The End

Playlist
Listen on Spotify

"California Love" by 2Pac, Roger, Dr. Dre

"Big Poppa" by The Notorious B.I.G.

"No Diggity" by Blackstreet, Dr. Dre, Queen Pen

"Would?" by Alice in Chains

"Burden In My Hand" by Soundgarden

"Creep" by Radiohead

"Better Man" by Pearl Jam

"Crazy" by Aerosmith

"Nookie" by Limp Bizkit

"Zombie" by The Cranberries

"Soul Suckin' Jerk" by Beck

"You Learn" by Alanis Morissette

"Your Decision" by Alice in Chains

"Pink" by Aerosmith

"I Need To Know" by Tom Petty and the Heartbreakers

"Lithium" by Nirvana

"Polly" by Nirvana

"Big Time Sensuality" by Björk

"The End" by The Doors

Dear Reader,

We hope you enjoyed this book and thank you for taking the time to leave a review! If you're wondering, K Webster wrote Will's chapters and J.D. Hollyfield wrote Lil's. We had a blast writing this story! Hope you check out our other projects as well! You don't want to miss out on the 2 Lovers series we co-wrote together! It's sexy and hilarious—full of wild shenanigans!

If you want to have more fun with us, come find us in our active reader groups on FB. We like popping into each other's groups and harassing each other from time to time (legit always)! See ya there!

K&J

K Webster's reader group, join:
www.facebook.com/groups/krazyforkwebstersbooks

J.D. Hollyfield's reader group, join:
www.facebook.com/groups/1513858735533272

More by
K WEBSTER AND J.D. HOLLYFIELD...

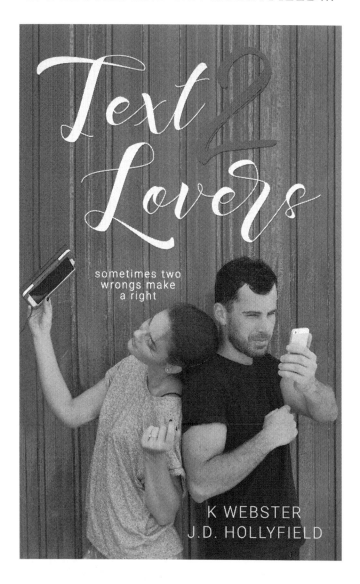

Text 2 Lovers

sometimes two
wrongs make
a right

K WEBSTER
J.D. HOLLYFIELD

Text 2 Lovers (2 Lovers Series, #1)

It's the start of nothing good.

I fired off a storm of raunchy text messages…to the wrong number.

And he replied.

Him: Show me a picture.

Him: Tell me your name.

Why does the lure of anonymity have me craving to indulge a stranger?

It's the start of everything right.

I received a slew of text messages…when everything in my life was wrong.

And she made me laugh again.

Her: You're probably a creeper.

Her: Possibly a stalker.

Why do I have the overwhelming need to find this stranger who saved me and make her mine?

Him: Take a chance with me.

Her: This is crazy.

Him: I need to see you.

Her: What are we doing?

Him: We're about to find out.

Her: PHOTO ATTACHED

Him: PHOTO ATTACHED

Hate 2 Lovers
hate isn't the only four-letter word to describe what they have
K WEBSTER
J.D. HOLLYFIELD

Hate 2 Lovers (2 Lovers Series, #2)

She hates him and his big head.
He likes her and her big t*ts.

She hates him because she somehow ends up naked every time she sees him.
He likes her because she somehow ends up naked every time he sees her.

She hates him because the big oaf knocked her up with his kid.
He likes her because she's carrying his child.

She hates the way he gets inside her head.
He likes the way she lets him see glimpses of her heart.

Andie: I hate you.
Roman: I know…but I'm going to change that.

Thieves 2 Lovers

being bad
never felt
so good

K WEBSTER
J.D. HOLLYFIELD

Thieves 2 Lovers (2 Lovers Series, #3)

Best friends aren't supposed to kiss.
But these best friends did.

He can't get the taste of her lips off his mind.
She can't let go of the guilt from her mistake.

He wants to be good enough for her.
She wishes life were different.

He's the bad boy reject.
She's the girl next door.

When opposites attract, they collide and create an explosion
that can't be ignored.
Is it possible to be madly in love with your best friend?

Love follows no rules because love is a rebel.

Her: We should talk about what's happening...
Him: It's about damn time.

Acknowledgements from
K WEBSTER

A huge thank you to my boo, Jessica Hollyfield. I love you like a sister! I'm so glad we became friends! Now, you'll never get rid of me…

Thank you to my husband. You're amazing. I love you more than I could ever truly express.
A huge thank you to my Krazy for K Webster's Books reader group. You all are insanely supportive and I can't thank you enough.

A gigantic thank you to my betas who read this story. You all helped make this story even better. Your feedback and early reading is important to this entire process and I can't thank you enough.

A giant thank you to Misty Walker for reading this story along the way and encouraging me!

Thank you to Jillian Ruize, Nikki Ash, and Gina Behrends for proofreading this book and being such supportive friends. Your eagle eyes are amazing!! You ladies rock!!

A huge shout out to my sister Holly Sparks! You're an awesome lady, a great supporter, and a whiz when it comes to keeping me organized. I appreciate and love you!

A big thank you to my author friends who have given me your friendship and your support. You have no idea how much that means to me.

Thank you to all of my blogger friends both big and small that go above and beyond to always share my stuff. You all rock! #AllBlogsMatter

Emily A. Lawrence, thank you SO much for editing this book. You're a rock star and I can't thank you enough! Love you!

Thank you Stacey Blake for being amazing as always when formatting my books and in general. I love you! I love you! I love you!

A big thanks to my PR gal, Nicole Blanchard. You are fabulous at what you do and keep me on track!

Lastly but certainly not least of all, thank you to all of the wonderful readers out there who are willing to hear my story and enjoy my characters like I do. It means the world to me!

Acknowledgements from
J.D. HOLLYFIELD

First, and most importantly, I'd like to thank Uncle Tom and Aunt Cherie. Thank you for approaching me with this fun idea. Giving life to this concept, K and I had so much fun putting it in words. Thanks to you both and your creative imagination! Sundays are definitely for hangovers and appreciation.

To Kristi, my wingman. My creative partner in crime. You're like a fine wine. You get doper with age. Thank you for being amazing, real, and downright magically delicious (okay I might be eating a bowl of lucky charms while writing this). These journeys that we take together have been some of the funniest moments of my entire writing career. Let's keep this shit up. To many more laughs, cries and back door arguments.

It wouldn't be a proper acknowledgements if I didn't thank myself. It's not easy having to drink all the wine in the world and sit in front of a computer writing your heart out, drinking your liver off and crying like a buffoon because part of the job is being one with your characters. You truly are amazing and probably the prettiest person in all the land. Keep doing what you're doing.

Thanks to my husband who supports me, but also thinks I should spend less time on the computer and more time doing my own laundry.

Thanks to all my eyes and ears. Having a squad who has your back is of the utmost importance when creating a masterpiece. From betas, to proofers, to PA's to my dog, Jackson, who just got me when I didn't get myself, thank you. This success is not a solo mission. It comes with an entourage of awesome people who got my back. So, shout out to Amy Wiater, Ashley Cestra, Jenny Hanson, Amber Higbie, Amy Khel, Kara Burr Orosz and anyone who I may have forgotten! I appreciate you all!

Thank you to Emily at Lawrence Editing for helping bring this story to where it needed to be.

Thank you to All By Design for creating my amazing cover. A cover is the first representation of a story and she nailed it.

Thank you to my awesome reader group, Club JD. All your constant support for what I do warms my heart. I appreciate all the time you take in helping my stories come to life within this community.

Thank you to Emilie and the team at InkSlinger and Nicole at Indiesage for all your hard work in promoting this book!

And most importantly every single reader and blogger! THANK YOU for all that you do. For supporting me, reading my stories, spreading the word. It's because of you that I get to continue in this business. And for that I am forever grateful.

Cheers. This big glass of wine is for you.

About
K WEBSTER

K Webster is the *USA Today* bestselling author of over fifty romance books in many different genres including contemporary romance, historical romance, paranormal romance, dark romance, romantic suspense, taboo romance, and erotic romance. When not spending time with her hilarious and handsome husband and two adorable children, she's active on social media connecting with her readers.

Her other passions besides writing include reading and graphic design. K can always be found in front of her computer chasing her next idea and taking action. She looks forward to the day when she will see one of her titles on the big screen.

Join K Webster's newsletter to receive a couple of updates a month on new releases and exclusive content. To join, all you need to do is go here (www. authorkwebster.com).

Facebook: www.facebook.com/authorkwebster
Blog: authorkwebster.wordpress.com
Twitter: twitter.com/KristiWebster
Email: kristi@authorkwebster.com
Goodreads: www.goodreads.com/user/show/10439773-k-webster
Instagram: instagram.com/kristiwebster

About
J.D. HOLLYFIELD

J.D. Hollyfield is a creative designer by day and superhero by night. When she's not cooking, event planning, or spending time with her family, she's relaxing with her nose stuck in a book. With her love for romance, and her head full of book boyfriends, she was inspired to test her creative abilities and bring her own stories to life. Living in the Midwest, she's currently at work on blowing the minds of readers, with the additions of her new books and series, along with her charm, humor and HEA's.

J.D. Hollyfield dabbles in all genres, from romantic comedy, contemporary romance, historical romance, paranormal romance, fantasy and erotica! Want to know more! Follow her on all platforms!

CONNECT WITH J.D. Hollyfield

Website: authorjdhollyfield.com
Facebook: www.facebook.com/authorjdhollyfield
Twitter: twitter.com/jdhollyfield
Newsletter: http://eepurl.com/Wf7gv
Pinterest: www.pinterest.com/jholla311
Instagram: instagram.com/jdhollyfield

Books by
K WEBSTER

The Breaking the Rules Series:

Broken (Book 1)

Wrong (Book 2)

Scarred (Book 3)

Mistake (Book 4)

Crushed (Book 5 – a novella)

The Vegas Aces Series:

Rock Country (Book 1)

Rock Heart (Book 2)

Rock Bottom (Book 3)

The Becoming Her Series:

Becoming Lady Thomas (Book 1)

Becoming Countess Dumont (Book 2)

Becoming Mrs. Benedict (Book 3)

War & Peace Series:

This is War, Baby (Book 1) - BANNED (only sold on K Webster's website)

This is Love, Baby (Book 2)

This Isn't Over, Baby (Book 3)

This Isn't You, Baby (Book 4)

This is Me, Baby (Book 5)

This Isn't Fair, Baby (Book 6)

This is the End, Baby (Book 7 – a novella)

2 Lovers Series:
Text 2 Lovers (Book 1)
Hate 2 Lovers (Book 2)
Thieves 2 Lovers (Book 3)

Alpha & Omega Duet:
Alpha & Omega (Book 1)
Omega & Love (Book 2)

Pretty Little Dolls Series:
Pretty Stolen Dolls (Book 1)
Pretty Lost Dolls (Book 2)
Pretty New Doll (Book 3)
Pretty Broken Dolls (Book 4)

The V Games Series:
Vlad (Book 1)

Taboo Treats:
Bad Bad Bad
Easton
Crybaby
Lawn Boys
Malfeasance
Renner's Rules

Carina Press Books:
Ex-Rated Attraction
Mr. Blakely

Four Fathers Books:
Pearson

Standalone Novels:

Apartment 2B

Love and Law

Moth to a Flame

Erased

The Road Back to Us

Surviving Harley

Give Me Yesterday

Running Free

Dirty Ugly Toy

Zeke's Eden

Sweet Jayne

Untimely You

Mad Sea

Whispers and the Roars

Schooled by a Senior

B-Sides and Rarities

Blue Hill Blood by Elizabeth Gray

Notice

The Wild – BANNED (only sold on K Webster's website)

The Day She Cried

My Torin

El Malo

Sundays are for Hangovers

Books by
J.D. HOLLYFIELD

Love Not Included Series:

Life in a Rut, Love not Included

Life Next Door

My So Called Life

Life as We Know It

Standalones:

Faking It

Love Broken

Paranormal/Fantasy:

Sinful Instincts

Unlocking Adeline

#HotCom Series:

Passing Peter Parker

Creed's Expectations

Exquisite Taste

2 Lovers Series:

Text 2 Lovers

Hate 2 Lovers

Thieves 2 Lovers

Made in the USA
Columbia, SC
10 September 2021